"The police suspected Mor no proof. Every knife in tl ... accounted for and she didn't have a drop of blood on her. They gave her three polygraph tests, which she passed with flying colors. Of course, David and I were out of the question. You don't accuse little kids of whittling two hundred pounds of meat off their father's bones... flesh that was never found."

"That's horrible, honey." Glenda hugged him tightly. "Did they ever..."

"Find the one who did it?" Kevin unleashed a phlegmy little laugh. "I tried to tell them, but who was I? Just a kid with an overactive imagination."

"Who do you think it was?"

Kevin didn't want to tell her, but he gave in. "It was Mister Glow-Bones, Glenda. I swear to God, it was. He jumped down off my bedroom door, slid beneath the crack at the bottom of my parents' bedroom door, and he took my daddy away..."

Cover & Inteior art by Ronald Kelly
ISBN 978-1-63789-891-8
Macabre Ink is an imprint of Crossroad Press Publishing

For information address Crossroad Press at 141 Brayden Dr., Hertford, NC 27944
www.crossroadpress.com

First Edition

MISTER GLOW-BONES

AND OTHER HALLOWEEN TALES

BY RONALD KELLY

Copyright Information

"Mister Glow-Bones" was previously unpublished
"The Outhouse" was published in *Turn Down the Lights*, published by Cemetery Dance in 2013
"Billy's Mask" was previously unpublished
"Pins & Needles" was previously published in *The Sick Stuff* in 2009
"Black Harvest" was previously published in *After Hours Magazine* in 1989
"Pelingrad's Pit" was published in *Cemetery Dance Magazine* in 2010
"Mister Mack & The Monster Mobile" was published on the *Horror World* website in 2008
"The Halloween Train" was featured in Deena Warner's annual Halloween card in 2011
The essays "The Candy in the Ditch Gang," "Halloweens: Past & Present," and "Monsters in a Box" appeared on the Ronald Kelly blog *Southern-Fried & Horrified*

CONTENTS

Introduction

If you're reading this on a cool October night, we probably have something in common. We both love autumn and, most importantly, we both love Halloween.

No matter how old we get or how many years stretch between us and boyhood or girlhood, the joy and mystery of All Hallows Eve still lurks in our heart. You can still feel the sheen of greasepaint upon your face or the sticky trickle of vampire blood at the corners or your mouth, feel the weight of the trick-or-treat bag in your hand, growing steadily pregnant with Baby Ruths, Tootsie Pops, Smarties, and black-and-orange-wrapped peanut butter kisses. You can taste the sweet ecstasy of candy corn upon your tongue and the bitter tang of wood smoke and damp leaves in your nostrils. And you remember the shadows stretching between every tree and house, and the potential for fright they held in the most real and emotionally delicious way.

It was okay to be scared when you were a kid. It was okay to cower beneath your covers because you believed the Boogeyman had taken up residence in your closet or beneath your bed. It was okay to shiver and grin as you flipped through the latest issue of *Famous Monsters, Creepy,* or *Eerie,* or comics like *House of Mystery* or *Werewolf by Night.* It was okay to pretend you were a ten-year-old Dr. Frankenstein as you wielded model glue and Testors paint and brought forth plastic incarnations of Dracula, the Mummy, and the Creature from the Black Lagoon.

Even in adulthood, it is okay to be frightened. To sit in the darkness while your family is asleep, reading by lamplight, allowing prose to lift from the pages and turn into cobwebs and catacombs, monsters and murderers. And, as you are immersed in the magic of the story, feel gooseflesh stipple your arms and the nape of your neck, and believe you hear something creeping behind the armchair or couch; sneaking, slithering, scarcely breathing… or failing to breathe at all.

Halloween is more than a holiday; more than a fun time of candy and costumes for the young. It is inoculated into our very being at an early age and there it remains. As we grow old, it grows dormant… but it is still there. For the lucky ones, such as us, it emerges every year, like a reanimated corpse digging its way out of graveyard earth to shamble across our souls. And we rejoice… oh, if we are the fortunate ones, we most certainly rejoice.

So turn these pages and celebrate our heritage. Blow the dust off the rubber mask in the attic and hang the glow-in-the-dark skeleton upon the door. Light the hollowed head of the butchered pumpkin and string the faux cobweb from every corner and eave.

It's Halloween once again. Shed your adult skin with serpentine glee and walk the blustery, October streets of long years past. And, most of all, watch out for misplaced steps in the darkness and the things that lurk, unseen, in the shadows in-between.

— Ronald Kelly
Brush Creek, TN
October 2014
HAND WITH KNIFE IMAGE

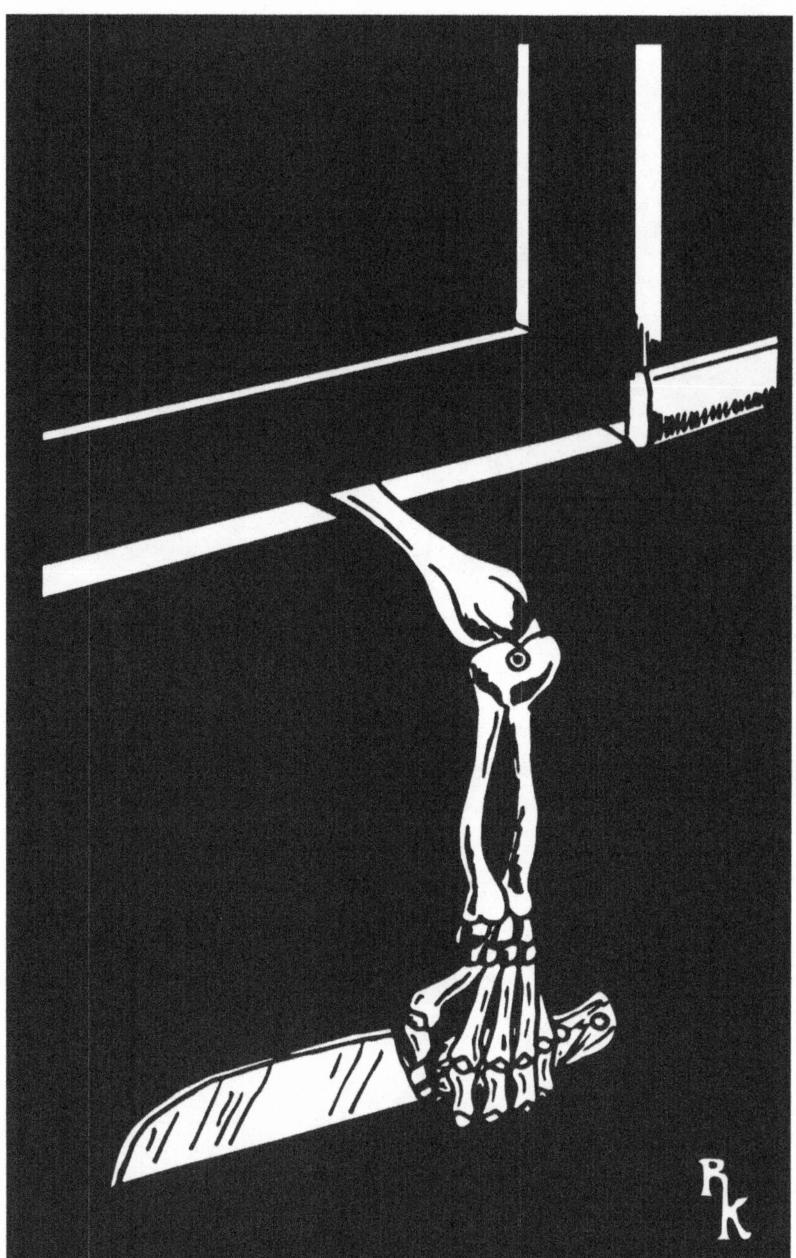

Mister Glow-Bones

"Hey, Daddy! Look at this!"

They were in the attic, rummaging through a dusty old trunk near the oval window. Much to Hannah's and Ethan's delight, they had come across some old Halloween decorations: a couple of rolls of orange-and-black crepe paper; faded cardboard die-cuts of ghosts, witches, and black cats; and assorted rubber critters—a bat, a rat, and several spiders.

When the five-year-old girl called out excitedly, Kevin Bennett glanced down into the bottom of the trunk. He felt a jolt run through him, as though he had just jammed the tines of a fork into the slits of a wall outlet.

It was Mister Glow-Bones.

At least that was what the cardboard and cellophane package had called him thirty years ago… and so had Kevin and his younger brother, David. LIFE-SIZED MISTER GLOW-BONES! GLOW-IN-THE-DARK! 5 FEET TALL! FULLY ARTICULATED! AMAZE AND TERRIFY YOUR FRIENDS! They had bought it at the Dollar General in Ashland City the October that their father had died.

Or, rather, had been murdered.

Stunned, Kevin stared at the decoration that filled the floor of the trunk, from wall to wall. The cardboard skeleton was silk-screened white, black, and phosphorescent green with hinged arms and legs on metal rivets folded across its ribcage and pelvis. Its eyeless skull grinned up at Kevin almost gleefully, as if saying "Howdy, kiddo! Long time no see!"

He couldn't help but shiver. He had been certain that Glow-Bones was long gone; lost or tossed in the garbage before they had packed up and moved to the city back in '84.

Ethan lowered the trunk lid until it was almost closed and peeked through the crack inside. The eight-year-old grinned. "Wow! It even glows in the dark!"

"That's impossible," Kevin told him. "It's been shut up in there for years."

But his son was right. He could see that eerie green glow illuminating the interior of the trunk, as though the skeleton had basked in the sunlight for days.

Hannah pushed the lid up and leaned down, nearly tumbling into the depths of the box. Kevin reached out and grabbed her hand before she could touch it.

"Don't!" he said, a little more sharply than he intended to.

Hannah eyed him questioningly. "Why? I want to hang him up."

"Me, too!" seconded Ethan.

"It's dirty… moldy," Kevin explained, not sounding the least bit convincing. "It's got a tear at its collarbone and the hole at the top of the head has pulled through. We'll run to Wal-Mart in the morning and get you a new one."

"But they've only got the crappy plastic ones!" Hannah said, pouting. "This is a lot creepier. Let's unfold it and see how tall it is!"

She tried to move her hand downward again, but Kevin held fast. "It's five feet," he snapped. "Now just leave it alone!"

The confusion in his daughter's eyes changed into fear. "Daddy… you're hurting my wrist."

Kevin let go. He felt badly when he saw the white imprints of his fingertips against her summer-tanned skin.

Just stop it! He told himself. *It had nothing to do with what happened!* But, in the back of his mind, he knew that was a lie.

"You can take the rest, but Mister Glow-Bones stays here."

Ethan's eyes widened. "Mister Glow-Bones? Is that his name?"

Before their interest could grow any further, he slammed the lid of the trunk shut and locked it with its skeleton key… which seemed unsettlingly appropriate.

As he hustled his youngsters back toward the trapdoor that led down to the hallway of the upper floor, Kevin glanced back at the trunk one last time… and was certain that he saw that muted green glow emanating from the depths of the keyhole.

That night, he sat on the front porch swing.

In the dark.

Thinking.

Kevin wanted to ask himself why the hell they had moved back to Kingston Springs, to the farmhouse on Willow Road. But the answer was unavoidable—they *had* to. A brush with bankruptcy after his long layoff had forced them to give up their apartment in Nashville and return to the old farmhouse he had called home for the first six years of his life. After all, it was his. After what had happened, he could never understand why his mother had kept the farmhouse and the forty acres of property that surrounded it. But she had. And it was left to him—lock, stock, and barrel—after she had passed away from cancer two years ago.

He stared into the autumn night and listened for crickets, but there were none. It was too late in the season. Twilight fell across the two-story house, cool and silent. Sometimes a dog would bark or a train would roar on its way to Chattanooga. But not that night.

He turned his head at the slap of the screen door. His wife, Glenda, stepped out onto the porch with two steaming mugs in her hands and a blanket folded in the crook of one arm.

"Want some company?" she asked. "It's chilly out here. I brought coffee and a blankie."

Kevin forced a smile. "Sure. Sit your pretty little butt down." He took one of the coffee cups. The warmth felt good against the palms his hands. "Kids asleep?"

"Out like a light." Glenda took a long sip and sighed. "Are you okay?"

"Sure. Why?"

She nestled against him and covered their legs with the blanket. "I know it's been hard for you… moving back here."

"Uh-huh," he mumbled. "More than you know."

"What put you into this funk all of a sudden? You've been doing fine since we got here."

Kevin thought of Mister Glow-Bones, sleeping comfortably upstairs in the attic trunk. *Tell her,* part of him urged. *She'll think you're nuts,* the other part countered.

But he felt like talking; a rare thing with him, as far as October of 1984 was concerned. "Did I ever tell you about that Halloween? Before we moved from Kingston Springs?"

"No, you've been annoyingly vague about it," Glenda said. "I'd like to hear about it, though. If you're ready to tell me."

I'm not, he thought to himself… then told her anyway.

"I was six years old… just a year older than Hannah is now. David was four. Daddy was farming then; tobacco and soybean, a few Black Angus on the side. Mama kept us in home-cooked meals and clean clothes. The ideal Southern family."

"Sounds like it to me," Glenda said.

"Well, it was. For a while." Kevin took a long draw on the coffee and felt it burn its way down his throat. "Then Halloween came in '84 and it all changed."

"The year your father died."

"Yes. A few days before, Mama had taken us to the dollar store in town to buy Halloween decorations. David picked some rubber bats and spiders. I picked…" He hesitated for a moment. "Mister Glow-Bones."

Glenda frowned. "That cardboard skeleton that you wouldn't let the kids have?"

Kevin turned and looked at her. "How do you know about that? Hannah?"

His wife nodded. "Little Miss Tattle-Tale. But I'm not going to fuss at you. I reckon you have your reasons."

"I do… and I'm getting to that." Kevin set down his coffee mug and breathed in a great lungful of cool Tennessee air. "Anyway, we had the house all decorated up. It was kind of pointless, though. We lived so far out on Willow Road that hardly any trick-or-treaters showed up. Mama stayed at home with a bowl of Smarties and Tootsie Rolls, just in case, while Daddy drove us into town to do our own trick-or-treating. I was dressed like Batman and David was a pirate, I think. We racked up. When we finally got home, our bags were about five or six pounds each.

"We changed out of our costumes into our pajamas and sat at the kitchen table to sort out our candy. You know, candy bars in one pile, bubble gum and suckers in another, odd things like apples, popcorn balls, and homemade cookies in a third. I remember Mrs. Adkins down the road gave us a toothbrush and a little tube of Crest that year. Just what two candy-eating boys needed."

"Sounds like quite a haul."

Kevin nodded. "It was. It was the best Halloween I'd ever had... until later that night. When Mama woke us up... screaming."

They were silent for a long moment. Then Glenda spoke. "How did your father die? You never told me."

Kevin opened his mouth, but his throat locked up on him. He took another sip of coffee. It tasted horribly bitter that time. "He... he was killed. He was murdered in his bed."

He could feel Glenda stiffen beside him. "Murdered? How?"

Kevin sat there, feeling weak and unsteady. *I don't think I can do this. I don't think I can tell her.*

But he did.

"I jumped out of bed when I heard Mama screaming. It sounded like someone had jammed a knife into her gut and twisted it, the way she hollered. I stepped out into the hallway... and heard the back door screen slap shut."

"Who was it?" Glenda asked him. Her slender hands held his arm tightly.

"I... I went to the window at the end of the hall and looked down at the back yard," he told her. "I saw a man walking away from the house, toward the back pasture." Kevin raised the coffee mug to his lips, but was disappointed to find it empty. "He... he looked like Daddy, but a little shorter, a little skinnier. He stopped, turned his head, and looked up at me... grinning. And his teeth... his teeth sort of... glowed."

"Glowed?"

"Yes, glowed... *green.* Like... Mister Glow-Bones. I turned and looked at my bedroom door. The nail on the top panel was still there, but..."

"Mister Glow-Bones was gone?"

Kevin nodded. Emotion began to grab hold of him then and his throat began to ache with the hurt of the memory. "And then I walked to Mama and Daddy's room… the door was open… and Mama was sitting against the headboard of the bed… her knees drawn to her chest… screaming and screaming and screaming…"

"And your father?"

"Was gone," Kevin managed. "Well, partially gone."

Glenda snaked a comforting arm around his shoulders and brought her head close to his. "You don't have to —"

"Yes, I do!" he blurted. "He… he had been… *carved* up. There wasn't anything but bloody bones. No meat or skin left to him at all. Whoever… *whatever* did it… took everything. Even his eyes."

"Oh, Kevin!" Glenda hugged him close to her, letting his tearful face wet the shoulder of her flannel pajama top.

"They… the police… thought Mama did it. Can you believe that? My sweet little mama? They said she couldn't have slept through such a slaughter… that she had to have taken a butcher knife from the kitchen drawer and carved him up like a Thanksgiving turkey."

"But they never charged her."

"They had no proof. Every knife in the kitchen drawer was accounted for and she didn't have a drop of blood on her. They gave her three polygraph tests, which she passed with flying colors. Of course, David and I were out of the question. You don't accuse little kids of whittling two hundred pounds of meat off their father's bones… flesh that was never found."

"That's horrible, honey." Glenda hugged him tightly. "Did they ever…"

"Find the one who did it?" Kevin unleashed a phlegmy little laugh. "I… I tried to tell them, but who was I? Just a kid with an overactive imagination."

"Who did you think it was?"

Kevin didn't want to tell her, but he gave in. "It was Mister Glow-Bones, Glenda. I swear to God, it was. He jumped down off my bedroom door, slid beneath the crack at the bottom of my parents' bedroom door, and he… he took my Daddy away. He just slipped into his skin and clothes and walked right out the back door, across the pasture, and disappeared."

Glenda sat there and held him, but Kevin could feel a change in her. The way she held him, comforted him, was *guarded.* There was a hesitation in her affection, as though she knew she was cradling someone that might possibly be deranged... or dangerous.

"You think I'm crazy," he said, his voice muffled and wet against her shoulder.

"No, of course not. You were a little kid. Little kids think strange things. You saw that Mister Glow-Bones was gone from your door and you blamed him for what happened to your dad." She pulled gently away from him and looked him in the eyes. "Did they ever find the one who did it?"

"No. They never did."

"And what about the cardboard skeleton? Did you ever see it again?"

Kevin's eyes were haunted. "No... not until today. In the attic."

Glenda shivered and stood up. "It's getting cold out here. Let's go in and try to get some sleep." She took both his hands and pulled him to his feet. "Thank you, though."

"For what?" he asked. He felt drained, emotionally and physically.

"For telling me."

Together, they went inside and turned the porch light off.

Later that night, in bed with Glenda snoring softly beside him, Kevin listened. Listened and heard tiny pops and creaks echoing from the attic upstairs. Sounds he wanted to attribute to the natural settling of wooden studs and floorboards.

But he knew better than that.

The next morning, Kevin stepped through his bedroom door into the upstairs hallway... and found himself face-to-face with Mister Glow-Bones.

The cardboard skeleton hung from a push pin on Hannah's bedroom door. Its arms and legs were unfolded and positioned as though it was dancing wildly.

"What the hell—?" Kevin stepped back, startled. "Hannah!"

When he got downstairs, he found Glenda in the kitchen, making pancakes at the stove. "Morning, dear," she greeted.

"Where's Hannah?"

"She's playing with Ethan outside. Why?"

Kevin ran his hand through his hair and sat down at the breakfast nook table. "Do you know what's hanging on her door?"

Glenda turned and eyed him. "Mister Glow-Bones?"

"How did you—?"

"He was laying on the kitchen table when we got up this morning, along with the other Halloween stuff. I just thought you had a change of heart and put it there."

"Well, I didn't."

Glenda set a plate of blueberry pancakes on the table and stepped to the back door. "Hannah… Ethan! Breakfast!" Then she turned and regarded her husband. "Kevin, please don't make an issue out of this. I know how you feel about that silly old skeleton… but it's just cardboard and glow-in-the-dark paint."

"So you didn't believe anything I said last night?" asked Kevin, annoyed by her condescending tone.

"Sure I did, sweetheart." She took butter from the fridge and syrup from the pantry and set them next to the pancakes. "But… you were six years old. Old childhood fears and suspicions can linger, but it's been thirty years. Maybe having Glow-Bones hanging around will help you face them."

"You don't understand—"

"No, maybe I don't." The expression on Glenda's face told him that she was a little tired of his irrational fears of a Halloween decoration. "All I know is that Hannah didn't go up to the attic to get the thing and it certainly didn't climb out of that trunk and walk downstairs on its own."

Wanna bet? he thought, but didn't say it.

"Just leave well enough alone and let the kids have their fun. Okay?"

At that moment, Hannah and Ethan burst through the back door, laughing. The five-year-old plopped into a chair across the table from where Kevin sat, beaming happily. "Daddy, did you see who was on my door this morning?"

"Yes, I did," he answered.

"Mister Glow-Bones! Ethan helped me hang him up. We made him look like he's dancing and waving. Didn't he look funny?"

Funny wasn't the word that immediately popped into his mind.

Those eyeless sockets and even rows of pearly and perfect teeth grinned at him in his thoughts… both now and back then.

Howdy, kiddo! Long time, no see!

The month of October passed quickly and soon the last week was upon them, with Halloween on Friday night. The kids were full of excitement, as children are at that time of year. After several tours of the Wal-Mart Halloween section, Hannah finally decided to dress up as a Monster High girl named Frankie Stein and Ethan chose Captain America. Both brother and sister had a say-so in what candy Glenda bought for the big treat bowl on the foyer table: mini-Snickers, Nerds, and Starburst fruit chews.

That night, Kevin took them trick-or-treating in a few neighborhoods around Kingston Springs, while Glenda stayed home with the front porch light on, in hopes of seeing a few trick-or-treaters darken their door.

Kevin parked the Grand Caravan and then walked the kids up and down the streets, up to his waist in witches, zombies, and miniature pro wrestlers. His mind was four miles away, back at home. He didn't like Glenda being alone in the house, way out in the boonies… with that thing.

A disturbing image came to mind. The scrape of cardboard footsteps sliding along the hardwood floor and Glenda turning to find…

Howdy, girlie! Let me introduce myself…

Hannah and Ethan were heading up the sidewalk to another house, when Kevin took out his cell phone and called.

"Hello?"

"It's me, hon," Kevin said. "How's it going?"

"Fine," she told him. "We've had three kids so far. You were right. It's just not worth the trip to take kids trick-or-treating this far out. How are the rug rats?"

"Having the time of their life," Kevin told her. "Hannah stumbled and scraped her knee, so you're sure to hear about that when we get home."

"Well, be careful coming home."

"We will. Love you."

"Love you, too," she replied and then hung up.

Kevin slipped his phone back into his jacket pocket just as Frankie and Cap walked up.

"What's this, Daddy?" Hannah asked, holding up something from her plastic pumpkin tote.

"Pop Rocks, baby. You put them in your mouth and they explode."

The girl's eyes widened. "Cool beans!"

Kevin looked at his watch. "So, are you guys ready to head back home now?"

"Just a few more houses, Daddy!" whined Hannah. "Please!"

Kevin couldn't help but smile. "Okay. Just a few more."

Laughing, the two ran to the next house in line.

That night, Kevin lay in bed, unable to sleep. Every now and then he would glance at the digital display on the alarm clock on his nightstand. It was barely eleven forty-five. *Daddy died at midnight on Halloween,* he kept thinking to himself. *That's when Mama started screaming.*

He had his head propped up with two pillows beneath him. The bed was facing the door, which was open, revealing the dark hallway beyond. In the gloom he could see Mister Glow-Bones in gruesome green relief against the blackness. His arms and legs were positioned the same way as before. And he was grinning. Always grinning.

This is stupid, he told himself. *Just turn over and go to sleep.*

Kevin was about to do just that, when the skeleton's right arm dropped from its waving position and fell to its side.

His heart began to pound as he stared hard into the darkness, trying to detect any further motion. For a long moment it stayed stationary, pinned to Hannah's door the way it had for two weeks. Then the left arm swung slowly toward the sharp flare of its pelvic bone. That time it wasn't a sudden drop due to downward momentum. No, that time it was slow and deliberate.

Silently, Kevin turned his bedcovers aside and sat up, swinging his legs over the side of the bed. He peered into the shadowy corridor, wondering if he was simply seeing things or if he was dreaming. Neither proved true. With a tip of its hairless, skinless head, Mister Glow-Bones pulled loose from the push pin and dropped to the floor. He didn't end up in a limp pile on the floor, but stood erect, balanced on the thin edge of its cut-out cardboard feet.

Oh God, oh God, oh God, no!

Glow-Bones stared at him through the doorway for a long moment and Kevin was certain that it would start toward him, passing through the doorway and entering the master bedroom. But it didn't. Instead, the skeleton slipped to the side out of sight… heading in the direction of the staircase.

Quietly, Kevin stood up, feeling shaky and unbalanced. He slid open the top drawer of the nightstand and felt around until he found a flashlight.

"Ummm," mumbled Glenda. She lifted her head a few inches off her pillow. "What're you doing?"

"Go back to sleep," Kevin told her.

"What's the matter?"

He hesitated, then said, "I think someone's in the house."

That roused Glenda from her drowsiness. Alert, she sat up in bed, peering into the darkness. "What? Where?"

"Lower your voice. Downstairs, I think." He clicked on the flashlight and directed a pale circle of light toward the open doorway. Hannah's door stood unadorned on the opposite side of the hallway. The push pin was still embedded in the upper panel.

He heard Glenda grappling for something on her nightstand and the bright square of her iPhone screen suddenly lit up. "I'll call nine-one-one," she hissed from her side of the bed.

Oh, yeah, sure, thought Kevin. *Hello, police? Could you please send someone to 33 Willow Road? There's a Halloween decoration on the loose. It goes by the name of Mister Glow-Bones.*

Kevin directed his light toward his wife, causing her to squint against the brilliance. "Don't call just yet," he said. "I'm going down to check it out."

"Don't you dare—!" Glenda started.

"I'll be okay." He told her, then stepped into the hallway and pulled the door securely closed. A metallic click told her that he had locked the door behind him.

Glenda listened and heard his footsteps creaking down the hallway, heading for the stairs. *Of all the macho bullshit,* she thought. Then, after a moment's hesitation, she unlocked the keypad and dialed nine-one-one. *I'm not sitting here and letting you get yourself shot by some stupid burglar!*

She could hear a ringing on the other end of the line, then a crisp click as the receiver was picked up.

"Police..." she whispered harshly.

But the police did not answer.

Instead, a strange crackling sounded in her ear. At first, she thought it was static... perhaps a bad cellular connection going through.

Then she recognized it for what it was.

The brittle rattling of naked bones.

As he made his way down the risers of the stairs, Kevin caught a glimpse of glowing green in motion downstairs. The illumination crossed the floor of the foyer and ducked through the doorway that led to the kitchen. He directed the beam of his flashlight in that direction, but found nothing.

He was crossing the foyer himself, when he heard a clattering noise ahead of him. *This isn't happening,* he told himself. *You're just dreaming all of this.* But the coolness of the hardwood floor against the soles of his bare feet and the almost painful pounding of his heart in his chest told him that he was very much awake.

When he entered the kitchen, he found that one of the counter drawers had been slid open.

It was the utensil drawer. Where Glenda kept the knives.

As quietly as possible, Kevin crossed the kitchen floor. He flashed the light's beam into the tray of the drawer. It took him a moment before he realized that only one object was missing... a long-bladed butcher knife. Swinging the beam of the flashlight toward the far side of the kitchen, he found that the back door was standing open. Hesitantly, he walked to the screen door and stepped outside, onto the rear porch.

Across the leaf-strewn expanse of the back yard was a trail of glowing footprints.

Kevin stepped off the porch. Ignoring the chill of the late October night, he walked a dozen steps or more into the dewy grass. He knelt and reached out to the first footprint, which was small and slender and bony. As his fingertips moved to touch it, the blotch of pale green luminescence slowly faded and was gone.

Somewhere, inside the house, he heard someone laugh.

It tricked me!

As quickly as possible, Kevin turned and ran back to the house. He burst into the kitchen, made his way to the foyer, and then bounded up the stairs. When he reached the upper landing, he directed the beam of the flashlight down the hallway.

The corridor was empty. His bedroom door was still shut.

But something was wrong... at the base of the door. Near the crack between bottom and floor, was a dark, widening pool.

Behind him, Kevin heard the front door latch disengage and the squeal of unoiled hinges.

He turned, knowing exactly what he would find.

Glenda stood in the doorway. She looked a bit taller than her four-foot-eight and much thinner than her one hundred and thirty pounds. Her pajamas hung off her frame like a shroud.

He took a step or two downward, but then stopped.

His wife's loose, rubbery lips parted and she smiled. Her teeth—small and perfectly even—gave off an eerie phosphorescent glow.

So long, sweetheart, said Mrs. Glow-Bones. *See you later.*

Then she was out the door and gone.

In a daze, Kevin mounted the stairs once again. He walked down the hallway and stopped in front of his bedroom door. He didn't wonder how the thing had gotten in. Something that was a sixteenth of an inch thick didn't have to turn a door knob. It simply slid through the gap underneath.

Kevin sank to his knees and found himself in the middle of a warm, wet puddle. He dropped his flashlight, then reached and picked something up from its sticky center. The object pulled away from the floor with a sucking noise.

He heard a door open behind him and slowly turned his head. Hannah stood in her bedroom doorway. She stared at him… at the blood… at the long-bladed butcher knife in his hand.

"What did you do, Daddy?" she asked him, frightened.

Kevin Bennett simply stared at his daughter, unable to answer. The true question was, what *would* he do? He wasn't an innocent six-year-old boy now, but a thirty-six-year-old man with blood-soaked pajamas and a butcher knife in his hand. A knife suitable for carving meat cleanly from the bone.

Outside, he was certain that he could hear the sound of distant laughter and the swish of running feet in the tall, dry grass of the pasture.

Feet that left a trail of pale green light in its wake, then faded just as quickly.

27
B
RK

The Outhouse

"Come on, guys. This is gonna be great!"

Frank Bennett and Bubba Cole looked at one another, their faces like pale masks in the October moonlight. They had no idea why they had let Mike Stinson talk them into coming way out there on the south end of Green Creek. Maybe they had just gotten downright bored with the way that Halloween night had progressed, kicking back a few beers that Mike had liberated from the little fridge in his dad's den, then rolling the yards of the high school principal and egging a few windshields from the overpass of Interstate 24.

The three trudged up an embankment, pulling themselves along by fistfuls of kudzu and the twisted trunks of small saplings, until they reached the top. They rested for a moment, winded by the climb, which seemed unlikely since they were the quarterback, a running back, and a linebacker for the Bedloe County Bears, state champions for three seasons straight. They figured it was the alcohol more than anything else that was slowing them down and Mike had gotten a head start on them before he had even picked them up in his Chevy S-10 pickup around seven-thirty that night.

Their fearless leader flashed that handsome, smart-ass grin of his—the one that had gotten him in a dozen fights and laid by a dozen girls during his junior year—and pointed across the rural stream to the top of an adjacent ridge of trees and bramble. "There she is, boys."

Frank clung to a sapling to steady himself and peered across the hollow to a narrow, wooden structure that stood perched on the opposite side. "It's an outhouse," he said, unimpressed.

"Hell, yeah!" Mike took the last long sip from a tall boy in his hand, then flung the can into the creek bed. "Tonight's crowning glory."

"Pushing some old outhouse into the creek is your idea of fun?" Bubba asked. His big moon-pie face frowned, puzzled.

"That's right."

Frank shook his head in disgust. "That's lame, man. Why would you get a kick out of doing that?"

"Because that's what country boys like us do," Mike told him. "It's, you know, a tradition. My daddy pushed over outhouses on Halloween and so did my granddaddy. And, as far as I know, this is the last one there is here in Bedloe County."

Bubba looked around. "Hey, ain't this Old Man Chamber's property?"

Mike nodded. "It sure is."

"Un uh," protested Frank. "You can just drive me home. I ain't messing with that old fart. Everybody knows since his wife ran off and left him, he's turned meaner than a rattler with a belly rash. Keeps that Remington 1100 loaded with double-ought buck and lead slugs, and he ain't shy about using it on trespassers, either."

"Quit being such a pussy," said Mike. "We'll push his crapper into the creek and be on our way before he can even hop out of bed and pull his britches on."

"I don't know, Mike…" Bubba grumbled, doubtfully.

"Oh, so you have my back on the gridiron, but you go chicken-shit on me when it comes to this?" Mike brushed his blond hair out of his eyes and looked wounded. "That hurts me. Deeply."

Frank and Bubba looked at one another. They didn't much like Mike questioning their loyalty, on or off the football field.

"Okay, okay!" Frank finally said. "Let's get it over with and get outta here."

"Knew you boys would see it my way." With a triumphant grin, Mike led them down the slope of the embankment, across the creek, and up the opposite bank. By the time they made the steep grade, they were nearly out of breath.

The three stood and regarded the outhouse. It was about six-and-a-half feet tall and five feet wide, constructed of weathered lumber and a roof of rusty corrugated tin. The hinged door had the traditional crescent moon carved in the upper panel. It was completely unremarkable, except for one thing. There was a heavy length of rusty logging chain wrapped four times around the circumference of the structure, secured by a big Yale padlock.

As they stood there, something inside moved.

"Damn!" Bubba jumped back a couple of steps. "Somebody's in there!"

Mike rolled his eyes. "Right… with all those chains wrapped around it? I know frigging Harry Houdini ain't in there, taking his nightly sit-down."

The big linebacker's eyes narrowed. "Who?"

"Never mind. Probably just a possum or a raccoon. Let's push it off into the creek and head out."

The three placed the palms of their hands against the eastern wall of the privy and gave it a shove. Nothing happened. It didn't budge. "Again," said Mike. They tried a second time. The boards creaked a little, but, still, it failed to move an inch.

"This old toilet is built like a brick shithouse," said Frank. "What'd Old Man Chambers do? Put a concrete foundation underneath it or something?"

"Bubba alone ought to be able to push this thing over," Mike said in irritation. He eyed the big boy. "Put your back into it, hoss. Just pretend it's Calhoun County's pretty-boy quarter and tackle the hell out of it."

"Okay." Mike had known exactly which button to push; he knew Bubba hated Troy Andrews of the Calhoun Silver Tigers, who was an even bigger asshole than Mike, if that was humanly possible. Bubba put his beefy shoulder against the corner of the outhouse, dug into the mossy ground with his feet, and pushed with all his might, his giant face grown red with the strain.

Wood began to pop and crack as whatever secured the privy to the ground began to give way.

"Do it, man!" urged Mike, laughing. "Get 'er done!"

"Keep your voice down!" warned Frank. He looked

nervously up the dark pathway that lead in the direction of the Chambers farm. "The old man will hear you!"

"Let him!" snapped the half-drunk quarterback. "I'll kick his shriveled ass if he comes down here giving me shit!"

Mike and Frank watched as Bubba grunted and gave the outhouse a final shove. It tipped over slowly, then cart-wheeled down the embankment, crashing loudly into the rocky bed of Green Creek. It hit with an explosion of splintered wood and mangled tin.

In spite of the danger of doing so, Mike Stinson unleashed a hearty rebel yell. "Hell yeah! Search and destroy! Bedloe County Bears—One… outhouse—Zero!"

Frank couldn't help but laugh. "You just ain't right, dude."

The moonlight revealed what the outdoor toilet had been perched upon. It was a broad, flat bed of smooth gray stone with a wide crack in the center. Curiously, Bubba walked over and peered inside. Usually, in an old outhouse, you could see something through the toilet seat—maybe a pile of lime with toilet paper and a few random turds scattered across it. But there seemed to be nothing beyond the fissure. Only pitch darkness.

"What do you see?" Frank asked him.

"Nothing." He found a stone lying nearby and chucked it through the hole. They waited to hear the echoing report of the rock hitting bottom, but there was nothing. No sound at all.

"That's weird as hell," said Bubba. The big fellow turned toward them, shrugging his massive shoulders. "Must be some kinda bottomless…"

It was at that moment that Mike Stinson and Frank Bennett noticed movement behind their friend… where the hole in the rock gapped just behind his feet. Then, suddenly, the thing was squeezing out of the jagged opening and looming over Bubba, making him look more like a three-year-old toddler than a 310-pound steroid and corn-fed seventeen-year-old.

Bubba saw the shocked expressions on his buddies' faces. "What?" Then he turned around and screamed.

It looked sort of like a bat, except that it was pasty gray and hairless and two-dozen times bigger than any he had ever laid eyes on. The thing's white, sightless eyes stared blankly at him until he began yelling. Then it latched its winged talons deeply into his shoulders, ripping past the vinyl of his letterman jacket and anchoring into the meat and bone underneath. Bubba tried to lurch backward, tried his best to get away, but his efforts were fruitless. He was in the creature's grasp and going nowhere.

Mike and Frank watched stunned as the bat's massive, fanged mouth clamped over the crown of Bubba's crewcut head and bit down. There was the crunch of bone and a curtain of blood coursed down their friend's horrified face. Then, with a violent shake of its gray-fleshed head, the bat-thing ripped Bubba Cole's head from the column of his neck bone.

"What the hell's going on down here?" someone demanded.

The two surviving high schoolers turned to find Old Man Chambers marching down the pathway, dressed in filthy long johns, his white hair flying like dandelion fluff around his head. He held a Remington semi-auto shotgun in his liver-spotted hands.

When he reached the little clearing where the outhouse had once stood, his face grew deathly pale. "Oh shit! What have you done, you damn fool kids?"

Mike didn't seem the least bit inebriated now. Funny how fast you can sober up when one of your best buds is decapitated by some freaking, giant bat-monster. "What... what the crap is that *thing*?"

The three stared at the gray creature. It grinned at them, rolling Bubba's head around inside its mouth like a jawbreaker, before finally swallowing it.

"I don't know exactly what it is, son," the old man told him truthfully. "All I know is that it was safely trapped where it was, before you pushed the cap off that crack in the rock and let it loose." He spat to the side and lifted the muzzle of his shotgun, pointing it toward the thing as it struggled to squeeze the rest of the way through the hole. "Dadburned thing killed my wife and drug her down into its cave, lair, wherever, while she was sitting on the pot taking a dump and reading *Better Homes and Gardens*. I chained up the outhouse to keep it locked inside. Told everybody that story about her leaving me because, frankly, I didn't think anyone would believe me otherwise."

The thing was almost free now. Its right foot was caught in a narrow corner of the crevice, which looked as though it was growing wider with each moment. The pale bat-creature shrieked shrilly, nearly bursting their eardrums with its unholy resonance. It spread its lanky arms, displaying a wingspan that was every inch of twenty feet across.

"You boys get outta here!" hollered Old Man Chambers. "I'll try to hold them off as long as I can. And head down the highway toward the lake... not toward town."

"But... but..." stammered Mike.

"No buts! Move your sorry asses!" The elderly man began to fire the shotgun, pumping alternate rounds of double-ought buckshot and deer slugs into the thing as it unleashed its foot and lurched forward.

The two boys didn't wait around to see if he had brought it down. They leapt off the top of the embankment, landing in the creek with a splash. They scrambled up the opposite slope and tore through the dark woods, listening to the piercing screech of the creature behind them. Then the boom of the twelve-gauge stopped and Old Man Chambers began to scream frantically.

Oh shit! Thought Mike as he ran through the brush and bramble as fast he as could. *Ohshitohshitohshitohshit!!*

A second later, Frank ran past him with a speed that had led the Bears to victory, game after game. It wasn't long before the running back was a good fifty feet ahead of him.

"Hold up, man!" Mike yelled. "Wait for me!"

"Screw you!" his friend replied and kept on booking.

Mike felt pain stitch his side and he struggled to keep up. He had suddenly realized that Old Man Chambers was no longer screaming, when something spun over his head and landed a couple of yards ahead of Frank. It hit the ground with a wet thud and, in the moonlight, Mike saw exactly what it was. It was Old Man Chambers's right arm, severed at the elbow. It still clutched the Remington 1100 in its twitching hand.

Even in death, the old man's fingers reacted with fear and panic. His forefinger squeezed the trigger again and again, causing the shotgun to discharge. One blast sent a twelve-gauge slug slamming squarely into Frank's left leg, blowing it completely off at the kneecap. As Frank fell, another blast peppered his abdomen with double-ought buckshot. The pellets pierced the muscles of his belly and lodged deep within his guts.

The disembodied arm spun on the ground and, in the process, began to fire impotently into the darkness of the surrounding forest. Mike continued to run and leapt over his fallen friend without a second thought. He continued to run for the edge of the woods and Highway 70 just beyond.

"Come back here, Mike, you son of a bitch!" wailed Frank behind him. "Don't leave me here!"

The bat-thing screeched again, much closer than a moment ago.

"Screw you, Frank!" Mike called back and kept on running. He glanced over his shoulder once and saw his friend lying, crippled and gut shot, in the autumn leaves. That and something huge and hungry and as pale and gray as newly-poured concrete lurching through the trees at an alarming pace.

Mike sprinted a few yards farther, then abruptly found himself out of the woods and sliding on the loose gravel of the shoulder of the road. He regained his balance and ran across the two-lane highway to where his pickup truck was parked. As he reached the vehicle and wrenched the door open, he heard Frank's bloodcurdling screams begin to rise into the cool night air.

He slammed the door and was comforted to find the key still in the ignition, left there for a speedy escape following their midnight escapade. He cranked the truck's engine into life and stomped on the gas.

As he pulled onto the highway, Chambers's instructions echoed in his mind. *Head down the highway toward the lake... not toward town.*

"The hell with you, old man," Mike said. "I'm heading home!"

He heard Frank scream again, but strangely, his shrieks seemed to come from above than from behind. A moment later, warm blood began to rain upon the truck, splattering the windshield.

Mike turned on his wipers, but they only smeared gore across the glass, obscuring his vision. Then beyond the red haze, in the swath of the Chevy's headlights, he saw the thing land on the center line of the highway. Clutched in the claws of its feet was the armless, legless torso of Frank Bennett. The boy was still alive, still shrieking hysterically, the flesh was peeled away from his scalp and face, leaving a wide-eyed, screaming skull in their place.

He jammed the gas pedal to the floor and sent the big truck barreling into the bat-thing in the road. The grill hit the creature dead-center in its chest, pitching it over the roof of the cab, and into the long bed in the back. The truck lurched precariously, nearly flipping as it continued onward, crushing poor Frank beneath its tires. Mike fought with the wheel and brought the truck under control before it could roll. He eased on the brake and glanced through the rear window. In the glow of his taillights, he could see the thing from the crack in the rock, struggling to lift itself from the bed of the truck. It looked battered and broken, but far from dead.

Frantically, Mike sped up, then slammed on his brakes sharply. The creature was propelled forward. It flipped over the top of the cab and landed on its back on the blacktop of the highway. The quarterback stopped stone still in the center of the road, then stamped on the accelerator, building speed. He completely ran over the thing that time. With satisfaction, he could hear—could actually *feel*—the bat creature's bones and cartilage breaking and shattering beneath the weight of the pickup truck.

After the truck had cleared its obstruction, Mike stopped and, through the blood-streaked windshield, saw the pale-fleshed creature lying in the road, utterly motionless. The boy sighed in relief. He sent the truck forward again, steering past the thing, as well as the silent, bleeding hunk of torn meat and bone that was once his best friend.

As he drove past a sign that read WELCOME TO COLEMAN and headed down a steep slope toward his hometown, Mike Stinson wondered if a trip to the carwash would eradicate all traces of that night's bloody outcome and if he would be able to sneak into his bed without his father being aware of exactly what had transpired.

Behind him, in the distance, he thought he heard an ear-piercing shriek.

Impossible, he told himself. *The thing's dead. I saw it die!*

But, as he drove onward, toward the outskirts of Coleman, Old Man Chambers's words came back to haunt him once again.

Head down the highway toward the lake… not toward town.

I'll try to hold them off as long as I can.

Mike's blood ran cold.

Them.

As the screeching, both urgent and hungry, grew louder and louder, he looked in his rear view mirror… and saw the moon turn black as the hole beneath the outhouse gave birth to horrors once forgotten… but no longer contained.

Billy

Billy's Mask

Brandon Halcomb glanced over the boy's shoulder as he walked by his desk. He stopped in his tracks and took another look. "What is *that*?"

"Uh... nothing," Billy Dupree answered self-consciously. His hand quickly slid over the drawing scrawled inside his wide-ruled notebook.

"Hey, guys, come over here! Take a look at what Billy drew."

Brandon's fifth-grade cronies, Trey Johnson and Jimbo Watts, walked over and peered over the nerd's shoulder. "What is it?"

"Move your hand," Brandon told him. When the boy refused, he reached down and roughly did it for him. "Look at *this*."

Trey's and Jimbo's eyes widened. "Dang! What is it?"

"Pretty cool, isn't it?" The bully leaned on the edge of Billy's desk until he was a couple of inches from his pasty, freckled face. "Is this your Halloween costume? Is this what you're going to be this year?"

Billy's oversized ears bloomed bright red. "Well, um, really it's..."

"I've got to see this for myself," said Trey. "Wanna go trick-or-treating with us tonight?"

"Yeah!" added Jimbo. "We'll meet at your house around 6:30."

Brandon smiled in that slimy reptilian way of his. "Okay, that's what we'll do. We'll meet at your house and take a look at this creepy mask of yours." He tapped the pencil drawing for emphasis. "But if you're pulling our leg, you little turd, I'm gonna beat the snot of you. Understand?"

The boy swallowed nervously. "Uh, yeah. Okay."

As the three headed for the classroom door, Billy quickly closed the cover of his spiral notebook before anyone else could see what he had been doodling.

"Where is he?" asked Jimbo. He was dressed like the pirate Jack Sparrow. "It's already a quarter till seven."

"I told you he didn't have a mask like that picture he drew," Brandon told them. He straightened his Dracula cape and adjusted his glow-in-the-dark fangs. "Now he's scared to come out here and face us."

"Wait a minute," said Trey, who was decked out as a flesh-eating zombie. "I think I hear him."

Inside the little white house on the corner of Elm Street, they could hear the boy's footsteps heading for the front door. "The guys are here, Mom. I'm going now."

"You be careful," his mother replied. "And watch out for cars."

Then the front door exploded open and Billy Dupree bounded down the front porch steps. He ran toward them with a paper shopping bag dangling from the crook of his arm.

The three boys backed up a few steps as he approached and the glow of the streetlight illuminated him.

"Shit!" declared Brandon, startled.

"Oh my God!" said Jimbo.

"Freaking awesome!" Trey laughed, shaking his head in amazement.

From his neck down, Billy looked like a regular boy. But, above that, his face was a decayed, crimson skull. The flesh that clung closely to the bone—which peeked out in sharp, yellow protrusions in places—was raw and the textured consistency of bloody red hamburger. His bright blue eyes—Billy's eyes—were set in dark, sunken sockets devoid of eyelids. His ears were nothing more than gaping, black holes and his lips were missing, exposing strong yellow teeth.

"Hey, guys!" he greeted with a skeletal grin.

The boys stood and stared at him for a long moment, then began to laugh. "It looks just like the picture in his notebook!" Jimbo said.

Brandon couldn't help but nod. "Yeah, I must admit... it is pretty danged cool, Dupree." He stared at the boy's left check, which was seething with tiny white worms. "Uh, do your parents know that you're playing around with maggots?"

Billy reached up and brushed the hungry larva away with his hand. "Oh... sorry." If he blushed in embarrassment, they certainly couldn't tell.

"Well, let's get going," suggested Trey. "You're going to scare the living crap out everyone, Billy."

"You really think so?" asked the boy, eagerly.

Brandon chuckled. "Hell, yeah!" he said, clapping the smaller boy on the back.

The four started through the autumn leaves toward the street, when they heard the sound of the screen door opening and Mrs. Dupree's voice rang out. "Billy! Come here, you silly boy. You forgot your costume!"

The boys turned and stared at Billy's mother. She stood on the porch smiling down at them, face glistening as raw as a wound, eyes unblinking, teeth stark white set in festering gums. A black centipede crawled down from her hairless scalp and disappeared into the long, triangular pit of one gaping nostril cavity.

"Aw, shucks... thanks, Mom!" said her son, scrambling back up the porch steps and grabbing the flaccid, rubber Billy mask out of her dripping and decomposing hand.

Pins & Needles

"There you go, kids," said Stephen Zachary. He tossed the last pieces of candy into the bags of the trick-or-treaters and smiled down at them. They were a cute pair, brother and sister. The girl was dressed up like a Tennessee Titans cheerleader, while the boy was decked out in an Incredible Hulk costume.

"Thanks, mister," they said in unison. Then they headed back down the sidewalk to where their parents' car waited on the Nashville street.

Zachary stared down at the empty bowl in his hands and his smile broadened even more. He closed the door, turned off the porch light, and checked his watch. It was only ten minutes after eight, but still he considered himself to be running behind schedule. He had quite a few things to do and a limited amount of time to do it in.

First he went to the kitchen to clean up. The Formica top of the kitchen counter was littered with paper and plastic; rat poison boxes, Drano bottles, and blister packs that had once held double-edged razor blades, thumb tacks, and sewing needles. He got a trash bag out of a kitchen cabinet and swept the litter into it, along with half a dozen empty Halloween candy packages and apple bags. As he tidied up, he remembered the long hours of preparation he had spent since awakening that morning. It had been fun—but meticulously maddening—especially trying to insert the razors into the apples without leaving a sign of tampering, as well as filling the little candy bars and peanut butter kisses with poison and pins.

Zachary went outside and, in the darkness of the back yard, dumped the contents of the garbage bag into the fifty-five gallon barrel that he used for burning trash. He took a can of lighter fluid from his coat pocket, squirted it liberally over the refuse, and then struck a match. He stood in the cool October night for a moment and watched it flare brightly. Zachary nodded in approval, then went back inside and prepared to leave.

It wasn't the first time he had done this. He had done it three times before, during the past twenty years. The last place had been Seattle in 2004. Seven kids had ended up dying and twenty-seven others had suffered painful – some disfiguring – injuries due to hidden razor blades, needles, and nails. He thought of the multitude of children who had rang his doorbell this Halloween night and wondered how many he would bag this time. He had counted closely and there had been ninety-two children in all, ranging from those barely out of infancy, to twelve and thirteen-year-olds. Zachary's largest yield had been in 1991, a grand total of sixteen dead and thirty-nine injured in Houston, Texas.

The thought brought back the smile full force. Ah, those had been the glory days.

Stephen Zachary didn't do it because he had suffered a lousy childhood. He hadn't been the fat or ugly kid that the other children had taunted and teased. He had no history of mental instability or past emotional problems that motivated that ugly hostility in him. He just hated kids, that was all... just like some people hated cats or dogs. He saw them in the same way as he saw insects; bothersome little organisms that provided only irritation and needed to be exterminated.

He had attempted to analyze his dislike for children many times, but had given up trying to rationalize it years ago. He simply derived pleasure from hurting children. Not with torture or molestation like some sick bastards did. No, he did it subtly with fruit and candy, passing out heaping handfuls of death and misery to tiny ballerinas, pirates, and a legion of superheroes.

Zachary walked into the bathroom and ran hot water into the sink. As he lathered his bearded face, he stared at his reflection and thought of the many changes he had gone through during a lifetime. Stephen Zachary wasn't even his real name, just like

Tom Haley and John Blanton had been well-planned aliases before that. He already had his next identity all planned out. In a few hours, Stephen Zachary would die and Roger Kirkwood would be born. The underground boys already had him set up. When he got to Baltimore, he would meet them in the backroom of a sleazy pool hall and receive his new credentials: driver's license, social security card, credit cards, the whole package. He had a new job lined up, a rented house in the suburbs, and a car with legitimate tags and registration parked in the driveway.

It had cost him a bundle—about twice as much as last time. But still it was worth it. He didn't get the urge to indulge in his secret passion very often, but when he did, the urge was uncontrollable. The extent he went through in order to escape punishment for his actions played havoc on his personal and professional life, but when he saw the dismay and horror on the network newscasts, along with footage of crying and bleeding trick-or-treaters, he always felt that it was well worth the trouble.

A few minutes later, the shaggy blond beard and mustache had been shed and he studied his new appearance in the bathroom mirror. His hair would have to be dyed darker, maybe black, but preferably brown. He could do that when he got out of the state. Just stop by a drugstore, buy a bottle of Nice & Easy, and make the change in a motel room by the interstate. The eyeglasses would have to go, too. He would start wearing contacts, even though they irritated his eyes. Maybe some of those new tinted ones. Yeah, blue eyes instead of muddy brown ones.

Zachary glanced out the bathroom window. The Lincoln with the U-Haul trailer hitched to the back was parked in the driveway, ready to go. The streetlights seemed a little hazy, as though a thin fog was rolling in. He checked his watch. It was nine-forty. The children were likely discovering their little surprises by now, sending their poor parents into a panic. It would be a while before a city-wide investigation was launched. He planned on leaving around ten o'clock. That gave him twenty minutes to wolf down a quick snack before he hopped into his car and headed north out of Tennessee. He found himself famished. He had been so involved in getting things ready for the kiddies, that he had neglected to eat lunch or supper that day.

He went to the refrigerator and got a quart of milk and a chocolate cake he had bought at a supermarket bakery the day before. He sliced himself a big piece of cake and poured himself a glass of milk, then sat down and considered the sensations that the little spooks were experiencing at that moment; the boiling pain of candy laced with drain cleaner in their tiny stomachs, the expulsion of blood from their mouths and nostrils as razor blades flayed the tender flesh from their tongues and inner cheeks, and the jagged jolts of agony that attacked them internally as needles, nails, and bits of broken glass churned through their digestive systems.

Zachary laughed, eyes gleaming behind the thick lenses of his glasses. He found his appetite even more ravenous than before. He took a bite of cake, then washed it down with a big swallow of milk.

Abruptly, he felt a raw pain in his throat. He coughed and wondered if he was coming down with the flu or something. His throat felt incredibly sore and inflamed all of a sudden. He took another swallow of milk. The discomfort in his throat grew even worse than before.

He dug into the slice of chocolate cake and brought the fork to his mouth. Zachary bit down and was surprised when hot liquid filled his mouth. A spray of blood shot from between the gap of his front teeth, splattering the tabletop with crimson droplets. A second later, agony gripped his lower face and there was more blood. A hell of alot more. In panic, he jumped up from his chair, knocking over the glass. Milk washed across the tabletop, along with dozens of tiny map pins, sewing needles, and sparkling fragments of broken glass.

His mind raced, wondering how the objects had gotten into the milk, but he found himself unable to think straight. The pain in his mouth was nearly unbearable. He poked a finger past his teeth and withdrew it quickly. The fingertip was cleaved cleanly in half, dribbling blood. *Oh God, what's going on? What the hell's in my mouth?* He glanced down at the chocolate cake with the single slice cut out of it. Double-edged razors winked with metallic malice from the layers of yellow cake within.

He ran to the bathroom and looked in the mirror. A single blade was wedged tightly between his upper and lower teeth, anchored securely into gum and bone. The blade was tilted at a downward angle and the rear edge was buried deeply into the throbbing meat of his tongue, which felt as if it were swollen to twice its normal size. He gagged, letting blood and pieces of chocolate cake fall into the sink. Zachary carefully tried to force his jaw wider, to relieve the stinging pressure and withdraw the razor blade, but to no avail. His jaw was already stretched to capacity. There was simply no way that he could extract the blade by himself.

Zachary knew that he had to get to the hospital. He was bleeding much too profusely and sharp pains had begun to shoot through his abdomen. He could imagine a swirling concoction of needles and glass slashing his stomach into bloody ribbons. *But I can't chance going to the hospital,* he tried to convince himself. *If I do, I'll get caught for sure.* His mind skipped from one option to another, but the pain that wracked his body was too strong and it was difficult to think things out correctly. He suddenly found himself not caring what happened to him in the long run. All he wanted at the moment was to put an end to the agony and the constant flow of blood.

He dug his car keys out of his pocket and stumbled toward the door. Soon he was outside in the crisp autumn night. The fog had intensified, growing heavier and more opaque. He groped across the small front yard, trying to find his car. Zachary located the front fender of the Lincoln and felt his way to the car door. He climbed in and started the engine. Then he snapped on the headlights and headed west toward the boulevard. He knew there was a hospital less than a mile from where he lived.

The fog was so thick that he had trouble seeing a dozen feet ahead. The headlights reflected off the heavy mist and blinded him. Despite his urgency, he found himself driving slowly. If he traveled any faster, there was a good chance that he might unknowingly swerve into the opposite lane or end up wrapped around a telephone pole, and that certainly wouldn't help his present condition any.

Fifteen minutes later, he spotted a lighted sign through the fog. Muted red letters proclaimed EMERGENCY. But something was wrong. It was located on the opposite side of the street from the hospital he had been thinking of. *What do I care?* he wondered wearily. *Just so they fix me up.*

He pulled up to the emergency entrance and parked his car. He stumbled toward the frosted glass doors. They opened with a pneumatic *swish,* providing him access to the waiting area of the emergency room.

Zachary could only stand there and stare for a moment. The place was packed. Dozens of children and their parents sat along the sterile white walls, waiting for their turn. The gathering looked huge. The corridor was long and narrow, seeming to stretch a mile to the reception desk where a couple of white-clad nurses sat.

He began the long walk to the nurses' station. He tried to avoid looking at the children as he passed, but still their bloody, pain-wracked faces invaded his vision. Some he recognized from that night, while others brought no recognition whatsoever. Many of the children had worn masks. Perhaps they had come to his door earlier that night and he didn't know it.

He reached the desk and tried to appeal to the nurses, but the blade wedged in his mouth made communication impossible. He could only grunt and groan. A squat nurse with black hair and cold gray eyes as hard as stones regarded him stoically. "Do you wish to see a doctor?" she asked.

Of course I do, you stupid bitch! thought Zachary, but he simply nodded to get his point across.

The motion sent fine beads of blood flying. They speckled the nurse's starched white cap, but she didn't seem to notice. "Please, fill these forms out in triplicate. Take a seat at the end of the line and we'll be with you as soon as possible."

Zachary stood there and stared at the complicated forms that the nurse handed him, unable to believe what was going on. He glared at the woman in angry protest, but she simply ignored him, going back to her own work. Zachary took a pencil from a cup on the desk and headed back to the far end of the waiting area.

On his way, he was again assaulted by the horrible faces of injured and dying children. Some were curled into fetal balls, while others writhed and spasmed in the concerned arms of mothers and fathers. He saw faces that he hadn't noticed during his first walk. They were vaguely familiar; the faces of children that he might have encountered on Halloween nights before, perhaps in Houston, Seattle, or Denver.

He turned his eyes away from those ashen faces with their shredded, bleeding lips and pain-glazed eyes, and stared down at the hospital floor. It was an inch deep with blood and vomit. Floating in the filth were needles, ground glass, and razors. They twinkled at him like sharp-edged stars in a violent and turbulent sky.

He reached the end of the narrow hall and found an empty seat. He sat down heavily and gasped out loud. His entire intestinal track felt as though it were being butchered from within, as well as his lungs. It was becoming difficult to breathe, but still the air wheezed in and out, whistling almost musically around the razor blade wedged in his teeth. He looked down at the insurance forms in his hand and shook his head in bewilderment. It seemed to be in some language he couldn't comprehend. His trembling hand jittered above the paper and, slowly, the pencil did a jerky dance across the forms, filling them out despite the muddled consciousness of his agonized mind.

He stared up, eyes pleading for someone to help him, but he found no one sympathetic to his misery. A small girl who was dressed up like Ragged Ann smiled brightly at him. She reached into a Halloween sack and took out a bite-sized Snickers. Zachary's heart leapt as he recognized the candy bar as one of those he had sabotaged. He tried to say something, but was physically unable to. He watched as the child bit the candy in half and swallowed it. Moments later, convulsions wracked her six-year-old body and a bubbling, white foam shot from her nose and mouth.

Zachary looked back down at the forms and found that they were all neatly filled out and completed. The dark-haired nurse walked up and took the paperwork from his shaking hands, which were jittery and black-veined from the poisons that coursed through his bloodstream. "Good," she said with a flat smile. "I see that you're finished. It may be quiet a wait, though. Due to the chaotic situation, we're calling all patients alphabetically, rather than order of arrival."

Alphabetically! his mind screamed. He gagged and gurgled, trying to talk some sense to her, but the effort only brought on an agonizing sneeze. A thick spray of bloody mucus erupted from his nostrils, staining the nurse's clean white dress with gore. Zachary stared at the fragments of broken glass and shredded nasal tissue that decorated the material. Again the nurse seemed not to notice. She turned and headed back to the front desk.

Waves of sickness and pain washed through him, and he watched in horror as the twinkling tips of a thousand tiny needles and nails forced their way from the pores of his skin. They skewered the flesh of his arms and legs, making it torturously uncomfortable to sit in the hard plastic chair. *I can't wait,* he told himself. *I'll die if I have to wait here much longer!*

He started to get up, but when he turned his eyes to the double door of the emergency room, he found that they were no longer there. Only a wall of stark white cinderblock stretched before him, blocking his exit. He turned his gaze back toward the narrow corridor. It seemed to stretch to infinity. The nurse station was so far away that he could barely see it.

"Next," called the nurse. Her voice echoed off the sterile walls of the clinic as if she were yelling from the pit of a deep canyon. "Andrew Abernathy."

He saw a miniature clown stand up a short distance away. As the kid headed down the corridor, he turned and grinned broadly at his tormentor. A profusion of bloody razor blades sprouted from the chubby cheeks of the four-year-old.

Stephen Zachary felt other small eyes, both living and dead, burning into him and he turned away, unable to meet their stares of gleeful accusation. He waited on pins and needles, knowing that an eternity of suffering lay between the letters of A and Z.

Black Harvest

"Well, there it is fellas," Elliot Leman said, gesturing toward a waist-high pile of newly-harvested corn. "Get it done by midnight and we'll have us a late supper and a barn dance that'll ring long and loud throughout these Tennessee mountains!"

It was an old-fashioned Halloween shindig and corn shucking just like they'd had back in the olden days. In fact, there hadn't been a decent shucking in Cumberland Valley for nearly fifty years. But Elliot's yield had been so plentiful that year that he figured, what the hell, might as well make a celebration of it for the entire township. The Leman family had done it up right, too, orchestrating the gathering to the most authentic detail. The menfolk wore flannel shirts and denim overalls, while the ladies came in knitted shawls and ankle-length dresses of calico and gingham. Coal oil lanterns hung from the barn rafters and jack-o'-lanterns sat atop hay bales, casting a warm glow over the nostalgic proceedings and putting everyone, young and old, into the mood for the hoedown to come.

Elliot stepped aside and the men lit into that pile of dried corn. They sat and peeled the shucks from the hard-kernelled ears, which they then tossed into a sturdy crib constructed of hand-hewn logs. Some of the women joined in, too, to speed the pace, while the rest prepared for the feast that would await at the end of their work.

One of those who took to shucking was Elliot's eldest son, Curtis, a strapping boy of eighteen years. Curtis was a senior at the local high school—a straight-A student and athlete who had hopes of winning a football scholarship and going away to college. He was an intelligent boy, Curtis was, but he had never begrudged his father his eccentric ways of farming; planting by the signs and such as that. No, Curtis enjoyed the ways of simple country living. He cherished the fellowship and warm feelings that abounded in his papa's barn that night as most of the tiny township of Cumberland Valley sat around the corn heap, just shucking and spinning yarns and tall tales, some of the men smoking cob pipes and chewing Redman tobacco.

Halfway toward the midnight deadline, Curtis yanked the brittle husk off an ear and, much to his surprise, found the kernels along the cob to be a brilliant crimson red.

"Well, will ya'll lookee there!" called out their neighbor, Charlie Walker.

Pete, the youngest of the Leman clan, laughed in delight. "Look, Papa… Curtis found himself a red ear."

"Let me take a gander at that, son," Elliot requested. He took the ear in hand and held it in the light of the nearest lantern. He turned it slowly and a big grin split his face. "Why, it surely is… a pure red ear. No spotted pokeberry corn there… it's plumb blood red, through and through."

"You know what that means, don't you, young man?" asked Grandpa Leman with a wink.

"Yes, sir, I sure do." Curtis blushed as red as his newfound ear.

"Tradition has it that you get to kiss the prettiest girl at the dance later on."

"Who's it gonna be, Curtis?" pestered Pete, nudging his big brother in the ribs. "Louise Varney or Emma Jane Betts? All the Abernathy girls are here tonight, each one of them prettier than the one before."

"It's my red ear, brother." Curtis grinned, sticking the corn into his overalls pocket for safekeeping. "I'll do the picking myself, if you don't mind. Anyway, we've got a heck of a lot of shucking to do till we get to that bottle underneath."

"Amen!" echoed several of the menfolk and, in anticipation, continued to shuck and toss.

It was a quarter till twelve that night when Elmer Baumgartner let out a hoot and a holler. In triumph, he withdrew a gallon jug of corn liquor from the midst of the dwindling pile. The jug was passed around until the very last ear was shucked clean and the celebration began. Everyone grabbed a china plate and piled it high with fried chicken, sugar-cured ham, and plenty of homemade fixings.

A few of the guys were warming up with fiddle, guitar, banjo, and mandolin, ready to pick a little bluegrass for the big barn dance, when Curtis finished his meal and joined a couple of his friends near the hayloft ladder. He surveyed the impressive abundance of pretty young ladies who gathered at the far wall, waiting to be asked to dance. He tried his darnedest to determine the loveliest of the bunch, but was constantly perplexed by the next one he laid eyes on.

Suddenly, he saw the one who fit the bill. She stood alone beside the open double doors—a shapely girl near his own age, dressed in blue calico trimmed in lace. Her complexion was like creamy alabaster and her long, waist-length hair was of a silky, raven blackness.

"Hey, fellas… who's that gal over yonder by the door?" he asked, mesmerized by her beauty.

"I don't rightly know," said Hank Tyler. "Never seen her before. She ain't one of the Harrison twins, is she?"

"Naw, both those girls have hair as light as corn silk," informed Teddy Dandridge. "That gal looks like she might have a touch of Cherokee in her."

"Whoever she is, I'm going over to ask for a dance." Curtis felt in his pocket for the lucky ear, then started across the spacious barn for the open doorway. Pastor Jones began to call a square dance, his baritone voice rising to the rafters. Most everyone there grabbed a partner and began to shake a leg to the tune of "Turkey in the Straw." In a far corner of the barn, some of the young'uns bobbed for apples in a big wash tub and played Pin the Tail on the Black Cat.

Curtis Leman mustered a charming smile and made his way through the milling crowd. The girl noticed his approach, however, and perhaps guessed of his intentions. She quickly ducked through the barn door and disappeared into the darkness beyond.

"Hey, wait up!" Curtis called out and followed. Stepping out of the warmth and activity of the autumn celebration and into the chill, motionless night was like crossing over into another world. He hesitated at first, thinking maybe he should find another girl from whom to receive his rightly-won kiss. But her dark loveliness haunted him. He continued on through the empty barnyard, past pickup trucks and cars, until he saw a fleeting movement ahead. The girl's playful laughter echoed through the night as she ran across the tattered ruins of his father's cornfield. He watched as a pale flash of calico flitted among the skeletal stalks, then vanished.

With a nervous grin, Curtis climbed the fence and entered the dark field. He pursued the sound of her footsteps and soft giggles through the maze-like rows, tripping over broken stalks and autumn pumpkins in his haste. A full moon etched the drooping, brown leaves in silver luminance, while the rutted rows of turned earth were swallowed in the shadow of the Smoky Mountains. The high swells of the range had always seemed to cradle Cumberland Valley like a babe nestled in the bosom of a protective mother. But that night, the mountains seemed cold and distant.

He had reached the center of the forty-acre cornfield, when he stepped into a parallel row and there she was. She stood as pale as a ghost, waiting for him.

Curtis was again stricken by her beauty, but the tedious hunt had sapped him of most of his bravado. He approached her, forcing the smile now. She did not turn to flee this time. She merely stood and regarded him demurely as he cleared his throat and stepped forward.

"I didn't mean to frighten you, miss," Curtis apologized. "I just wanted to talk to you for a spell." As he grew closer, he marveled at how porcelain smooth her features were, like the face of an antique china doll. Her eyes were dark and striking despite her apparent bashfulness. For a moment, they appeared as deep and bottomless as the black of her windswept hair. But, upon further inspection, they returned to their former hue of soft earthen brown.

"You did not follow me out here to talk," she said, almost in a whisper.

Curtis grinned clumsily and produced the red ear from his pocket. "If you're not familiar with the tradition…" he began.

"Oh, but I am… quite familiar," she told him. She eyed the crimson cob as if it were the jeweled key to some wondrous treasure. "In fact, it was my people who originated the custom, long years before this valley was even settled."

The boy's apprehension eased a little at that assurance. "Then you'll grant me my kiss?"

A cloud passed overhead, obscuring the moon, leaving her only in silhouette. "Most certainly, Curtis Leman."

He was surprised. "You know my name?" he asked. "I'm sure that I don't know yours. I don't believe I've ever seen you here in the valley before."

"*Who* I am does not really matter. It is *what* I am that is most important this night." She extended pale hands to draw him closer. "For you see, I am the maiden… the maiden of the Black Harvest."

What do you mean by that? he wanted to ask, but held his tongue. He didn't want to spoil receiving his intended kiss by asking stupid questions. A lot of the mountain girls were odd sorts, possessing a strange sense of humor that usually went completely over his head. But that didn't bother him as he started forward and took her dainty hands in his. All that filled his mind was her dark and almost savage beauty. He moved in closer, embracing her, staring deeply into the liquid pits of that strange girl's eyes. He found none of the shyness she had displayed before. Instead, there flared a sultry flame of total abandonment.

"Kiss me," she whispered, her lips lush and irresistible. "You've won the right… now claim your prize."

Curtis intended to do just that. He swallowed dryly and brought his lips in close proximity to hers. The hoopla of the fall celebration seemed to be a thousand miles away. It was a mere distraction in the wake of this lady's hypnotic charms.

When he found her lips icy cold to the touch, Curtis knew something was horribly wrong. He grabbed her slender waist to push her away, but the fullness of her calico dress seemed to crumple, as if the flesh beneath were slipping away. His fingers ripped through rotting cloth and slipped through the empty slots of her exposed ribcage. His knuckles scraped painfully against the pitted hardness of flattened bone, wedging there, denying his escape.

"Kiss me." Her lips moved like slivers of dead meat against his own.

Curtis tried desperately to pull away, but skeletal fingers clutched at him, dragging him nearer. A moan of horror rose in his throat as the lovely face of porcelain white seemed to yellow and crack with a hundred tiny fissures. The skin began to shatter and fall away like broken crockery, revealing stark white bone underneath. The sparkling brown eyes that had once smoldered with desire were now gone. Empty sockets glared at Curtis with an emotion akin to hunger, as the wretched thing pulled him closer.

Suddenly, he knew the meaning of her cryptic words. When Grandma Leman had fallen sick and passed away the previous year, Grandpa had sat before the hearth and, in a low, trembling voice, had said, "The spring has bled into summer and the coming of autumn has brought upon us a black harvest."

Curtis had never been able to figure out what Grandpa had meant by that… until now.

The Black Harvest marked the finality of one's existence; the crop of youth planted, tended to maturity, and eventually reaped, the same as a field of summer corn or a base of Burley green tobacco. There is a balance between Man and Nature, equilibrium. And when the scales tip too heavily in one an direction, compensation must be made.

"Kissss meeee," rasped the skeletal wraith. Her bony jaws clutched his lower face in a horrid kiss of eternal love.

Curtis began to scream wildly, his terror echoing through the hollow of ancient bones and the wind-whipped stalks of the deserted cornfield. But no one heard him. The sound of dancing feet and the rapid-fire staccato of banjo-picking drowned his weakened cries as the maiden lowered him to a bed of withered leaves and began to reap the ripened crop of that darkest of seasons.

TRICK
OR
1956

Pelingrad's Pit

October was the one month out of the year when Jake Abernathy was allowed to be himself.

Of all the holidays, Halloween seemed to suit him the most. Glow-in-the-dark skeletons on his bedroom door and a jack-o'-lantern grinning wickedly on the front porch steps. The meticulous planning of his costume… this year Count Dracula. Plenty of horror movies and those old copies of *Famous Monsters* his Uncle Jerry had given him for his birthday last year.

Still, that autumn, Jay felt oddly restless, as though something was about to happen that would ruin his favorite season and, perhaps, alter his love of All Hallows Eve forever.

When he felt that way, like the walls of his bedroom were closing in on him and his father's presence looming like an ominous shadow across his path, the twelve-year-old would head out the back door and into the woods that bordered the Abernathy property. Having no real friends to speak of, he always went alone.

There was a good half mile of forest within the basin known as Collin's Hollow, spanning between Three Forks Road and Highway 70. Tall stands of pine, oak, and cedar made up the stretch of woods, with dense mats of thick-leaved kudzu and dead leaves carpeting the ground. Jay found a strange peace and a sense of independence there in the sun-dappled shadow that he experienced neither at home nor at Coleman Junior High, where he did his time – and it *did* feel like an unjust prison sentence—as a bookish, introverted seventh grader.

Usually he wandered the woods, stopped halfway, and returned home before his parents even knew he was missing. But that afternoon in early October, Jay went a little further. He climbed the thicketed wall of the hollow's southern end and found himself only a stone's throw away from the main highway. He also found himself on the edge of someone's property. Jay was surprised—and a little disturbed—to find himself standing there, staring into the back yard of Old Man Pelingrad.

Viktor Pelingrad was an enigma in the rural farming community where he lived. The old man was nearly eighty and had lived on the outskirts of Coleman most of his life. His father, Eric, had moved to Middle Tennessee in 1937, along with his wife and son. Given the narrow-minded ways of most country folk, the Pelingrads seemed to have fit in with little friction at all. Eric farmed the pasture west of his little two-story farmhouse and Helga Pelingrad worked as a seamstress at a dress shop on the town square.

If anyone in the Pelingrad clan failed to fit in, it was Viktor. The boy had always been a strange one—quiet, solemn, always seeming to watch and listen, rather than speak. The kids snickered and made fun of him and his peculiar ways. He would keep a pet—a dog or cat—for only a short time and then they would simply up and disappear. Folks joked that the animals ran away from home, weary of their master's dark mood and utter lack of affection.

Viktor Pelingrad's demeanor hadn't improved with age. When his mother and father passed away, he worked the land and kept to himself, rarely conversing with the folks in town. He married in 1952, a lady from his native Germany named Lucinda. Some said that it had been the product of an arrangement Eric Pelingrad had made before leaving Europe. The union didn't last long, however. Lucinda up and left Viktor in 1956. Local gossip suggested that she, too, tired of Viktor's cheerless attitude and returned overseas.

Jay clung to the trees at the edge of the Pelingrad property, looking for a sign of the old man. Viktor's battered Ford pickup wasn't in the gravel drive at the side of the house, so apparently he was out running errands. Relieved, Jay stepped out of the woods and walked around. The elderly man's absence gave him the freedom to explore a place most of the kids at school considered taboo territory.

Viktor Pelingrad had been something of a boogeyman to the youth of Coleman for years. Nasty rumors of Old Man Pelingrad spread around school in hushed tones and creepy murder stories about him were told around the bonfires at 4-H camp. One boy in Jay's class, Andy Strickland, had even gone as far as spreading the rumor that Pelingrad was a Nazi war criminal, that he had been an assistant to Josef Mengele and had held down screaming children as the Angel of Death had sewn twins together and injected their eyes with blue dye. It didn't matter that Viktor was only seven when he and his family left Germany, Andy just kept perpetuating the myth. That was until Sheriff Biggs came around and talked to Andy's dad, who promptly put an end to the nonsense.

Now that he was actually standing there looking at the place, Jay found nothing of real interest within the quarter acre of Old Man Pelingrad's back yard. There was a rusty John Deere tractor sitting in high weeds to one side, the weathered hulls of an old outhouse and a long-abandoned chicken coop on the other. If anything drew Jay's attention it was a broad, shallow pit that lay at a distance from the house, close to the tree line.

It was a burning pit, something folks used to dispose of their garbage back before landfills became the norm. Some of the older citizens of Bedloe County still used them and the local authorities allowed it, just so the burning didn't get out of hand and bring the volunteer fire department rushing to put out a runaway grass fire.

Pelingrad's pit was about twelve feet in diameter and a couple of feet deep. Its rim was black and charred, while the middle was gray with ash and fire-burnished items that the blaze hadn't quite consumed. He didn't know exactly why, but Jay stepped down off the rim of solid earth and into the pit. Maybe he was just curious as to what he would find... maybe a clue as to the old man's personal habits—what he ate and drank, what sort of toilet paper he wiped his butt with.

The surface of the pit was hard and crusty. Jay felt it give a little under his feet as he walked. It was almost like pressing your hand against the papery wall of a hornet's nest. For an instant, Jay considered going back, afraid that he might break through. But to what? He knew all that lay beneath the charred refuse was more refuse. It wasn't like he was going to fall into some bottomless cavern under the ashy scattering of blackened tin cans and charred newspaper.

He walked to the center of the pit, looking around, prying bits of metal and glass loose with the toe of his sneaker. When he reached the very hub of the circle, he was surprised to find an old calendar embedded there, partially burnt, but still legible. It was from the Bedloe County co-op. Above the numbered grid was the year in broad, black letters. 1939.

"This can't be right," muttered Jay. "A calendar lying out here for… what? Seventy years?" He knew such a thing was downright impossible.

Then, as he looked around, he began to notice some other peculiar things, like glass milk bottles, baking soda tins, a water-logged copy of *Life* magazine dated the same year as the calendar. Sure, the Pelingrads would've probably burnt such things way back then, but they would have been buried deep *underneath* everything else… not lying on the surface, for everyone to see.

And there was another thing that was strange about the pit. As Jay stood in its center, the hard crust of ash beneath his feet seemed to radiate a *coldness.* A chill radiated around the boy that he shouldn't have felt on a warm October afternoon. He crouched down and felt the center of the fire pit. It was like touching the inner wall of a freezer.

But that wasn't all. Before he could pull his palm away, the crusty top layer of ash *moved,* heaving upward a half-inch or so.

Startled, Jay leapt out of the way. *Aw, quit being such a wimp,* he told himself. *It was just something burrowing underneath… a mole or a rat.*

A wave of dizziness swept through him and he stumbled. He felt disoriented and more than a little sick to his stomach, like he did after riding the Scrambler at the county fair.

Jay was turning to leave, intending to head back into the woods for home, when a sound drew his attention. It was a low, whimpering noise, sort of like a hurt animal. He turned and looked around, but couldn't locate its source at first. *This place is just spooking the shit out of you, that's all.*

Then the flutter of an old newspaper in the breeze caught his attention. He walked back toward the center of the pit and looked at the headline emblazoned across the yellowed paper. AMERICAN INVOLVEMENT IN EUROPEAN CONFLICT INEVITABLE it read. Another wave of lightheadedness gripped Jay and he lost his balance, sitting down hard in the ash. Suddenly the coldness he had felt before seemed to increase. He shivered and struggled to regain his feet.

That was when the source of the pitiful whimpering made itself known. The ancient newspaper moved as something underneath pushed against it. Jay didn't know why—he knew it was foolish to even do so—but he reached out and turned the newspaper to the side, revealing the poor creature underneath.

There, hidden beneath the paper, was a puppy. At first, Jay was certain that it was dead. Its sandy coat was matted and singed from flame, and its paws had been charred clear down to the bone. Rusty bailing wire was wrapped so tightly around the little dog's throat that it had burrowed deeply past the fur and into the flesh of its gullet. There was more wire on the puppy as well. It bound the animal's front and rear paws together, like a calf hogtied at a rodeo. The thing whimpered again, mournfully, full of fright.

"What happened, boy?" Jay whispered. "Who did this to you?"

It was at that moment that Jay realized that the dog was not breathing. Its sides, serrated with malnutrition and neglect, were still. And the puppy's eyes were glazed, staring fixedly toward the treetops at the edge of the Pelingrad property. As dead as dead could possibly be.

Jay felt bad for the puppy, which had obviously been tortured and thrown into this pit to burn. He reached out, perhaps to show his pity, to stroke its cold, unbreathing snout. "I'm sorry, boy," he said softly.

When his hand came within a few inches of the dog's nose, it lifted its head and licked his fingers. The puppy's tongue was gray and bloated, and as cold as piece of raw liver.

Jay cried out in alarm. Again he attempted to stand up. The coldness he had felt before reached a frigidity that made his bones ache. Frosty breath drifted from his mouth as he cried out and, finally making it to his feet, he took off and scrambled over the lip of the pit. Instantly, the cold sensation was gone. The warmth of the autumn sunshine returned, driving away the unnatural chill.

He stood there for a long moment, confused, unsure of what had just taken place in the basin of Pelingrad's fire pit. He looked for the dead puppy and the newspaper that had covered it, but found neither. The calendar was still there in the same place, but it now gave the year as being 2009.

But that seemed as odd and out of place as his encounter—or had it been a hallucination—with the dead dog. Why would someone discard a calendar before the end of the year was finished?

The crackle of tires on gravel drew his attention and he saw Old Man Pelingrad's truck pulling off the highway into the drive. Frightened, and more than a little shaken, Jay ducked into the woods and made his way quickly back down into the hollow just beyond.

His journey home was a frantic one, absent of the quiet pleasure he normally experienced during his ramblings in the forest. He tore through the thicket, his heart pounding, still disoriented by those few short minutes in Pelingrad's burning pit. Every so often, he turned and looked over his shoulder, feeling as though someone—or *something*—was close on his heels, following him.

But he saw nothing.

A week passed and Jay still couldn't get the dead puppy in the pit out of his mind. Most of it was the uncertainty of the entire encounter and the nagging doubt that it had even happened at all. There were the lingering aftereffects of what he had *felt* there, too. The dizziness, disorientation, and nausea that had gripped him so strongly in Pelingrad's back yard still remained, resurfacing physically every now and then. He mostly felt those troubling sensations at night, after a particularly vivid nightmare about the pit. He had suffered the dreams every night—dreams about the dead puppy lying in the basin of the pit, its charred paws wired together, its cold, gray tongue lolling from its mouth and that shrill, whining whimper echoing from a throat choked with phlegm and maggots. Once, Jay had dreamt that he had awakened and found the dog lying at the foot of his bed. The bailing wire was gone and its legs were unrestrained. Slowly, it crept toward him, clawing its way up the bedcovers, leaving a trail of ash and viscera in its wake. Its dead eyes held a sense of urgency to them, as though pleading, warning him to stay away from the Pelingrad place.

But that warning went unheeded. Thoughts of the puppy nearly became an obsession. He began to doubt his own sanity, wondered if he was going crazy or something. Sure, he liked to read horror novels and comic books, but he had never taken them to heart. He knew reality from fantasy. Or did he?

It was on the Saturday evening of the following week when he finally gathered up his nerve and decided to find out.

Around eight-thirty he excused himself from the family room, telling his parents he was heading off to bed. Pulling her eyes from the TV set, his mother smiled and told him goodnight, while his father, a high school football coach, merely grunted and ignored him as usual, immersed in a copy of *Sports Illustrated.* When he was younger, his father's indifference had bothered him a lot, but now he considered it a blessing. Cal Abernathy had eventually come to the sobering realization that his only son wasn't going to be the strapping football star he had been growing up. That was fine with Jay. He cared nothing about sports and the social bullshit that came with being a jock. All he cared about was his books and being left alone.

Jay had ducked down the opposite end of the hallway, heading quietly toward the utility room. He found a flashlight in a junk drawer and, tugging on a jacket, left through the door that led onto the back deck. He walked in total darkness to the edge of their back yard before snapping on the light. Then he carefully made his way into the woods and the dense thicket of Collin's Hollow.

The forest seemed much scarier and more treacherous at night than it did in broad daylight. In addition to his difficulty in navigating the woods, being unable to pick out familiar landmarks and such, there were nocturnal sounds that were totally alien to him. The hooting of an owl, the distant call of a whip-poor-will, and the scampering of things prowling beneath the thick carpet of kudzu and dead leaves. Once, he felt something slither past his left ankle, its rough hide snagging on the material of his sock for a terrifying instant before pulling free.

Finally, after what seemed to be an eternity, Jay found himself scrambling up the side of the hollow, to the edge of the Pelingrad property. He turned off his flashlight and lingered at the edge of the woods for a long moment, catching his breath and studying the old farmhouse. There was only one window lit as far as he could tell… in an upstairs bedroom. The lower floor of the house was dark.

Quietly, Jay left the cover of the forest and crossed the yard to the burning pit. There was no moon that night and, in the gloom, the pit was only a wide, pale circle in the earth. He glanced up at the bedroom window again, then snapped on his light and stepped down into the ashy basin.

The moment he placed his foot on the crusty floor of the pit, it all came rushing back to him. The dizziness, the nausea, that awful, bone-aching cold. He wanted to leave, but he didn't. He hadn't traveled that far in the darkness to simply abandon what he had come there to do. And that was to look for the dead dog that haunted him.

He reached the center of the pit and directed the beam of the flashlight at the discarded calendar that lay, embedded, in the jumble of burnt garbage. The date had changed again. It was neither 1939 nor 2009. Now the numbers above the dated grid read 1946.

Jay closed his eyes and breathed in deeply, then opened them again. The date on the calendar remained the same. He shined the light on the newspaper that had concealed the burnt and tortured puppy. Its headline had changed as well. It read HOUSING AND EMPLOYMENT AT ALL-TIME HIGH IN WAKE OF POST-WAR PROSPERITY.

Something else had changed about the newspaper as well. It was bulged in the center, as though now concealing something much larger than some poor, dead puppy dog. It moved as something pushed up weakly from underneath.

Softly, a baby cooed.

No, Jay told himself, rooted to the spot where he stood. *Just leave. Just head back into the woods and go home.*

The newspaper rattled as tiny, pale fingers appeared at the edge of the front page and shook at it. Again that soft, infantile gibbering.

You don't want to see this. Just go home and forget it. But he couldn't. There was no turning back. He had to take a look.

Jay took a couple of steps forward, then crouched next to the newspaper. His hand trembled as he reached out and peeled it away.

He found that he was more surprised by his discovery than terrified. It was, indeed, a baby.

The infant was maybe six or seven months old, dressed only in a diaper... and a *cloth* diaper at that, fastened together with a large safety pin. Jay couldn't tell whether it was a boy or a girl. In the glow of the flashlight, he could only tell that it had rosy pink skin, a tuff of honey-blond hair on the crown of its head, and blue eyes. Its appearance comforted Jay a bit. It certainly didn't look dead, like the body of the puppy had. It looked at the peak of health.

"What are you doing out here?" he whispered softly. A feeling of concern and growing anger came over him. *Who would do this to a baby?* he wondered. *Who would bring it out here to this pit and dump it here?* He glanced up at the window. It was still lit, the same as it had been upon his arrival.

Jay examined the baby more closely. As the baby reached upward, its tiny hands grasping for him curiously, he spotted the bailing wire, rusted and embedded in the soft flesh of each of its wrists. The wire was around its ankles, too, tying them together.

"Old Man Pelingrad did this to you, didn't he?" muttered Jay. He felt frightened now, for the welfare of the infant... and for himself. He had to do something. Get to a phone and call the sheriff.

The baby smiled up at him, blowing spit bubbles through

toothless, pink gums. It took hold of Jay's right index finger and squeezed. Normally this gesture would have been cute and endearing. But not now... not in the depths of the burning pit. The boy was shocked to find its grasp to be as cold as ice.

"Let go!" whispered Jay, beginning to panic. "Stop it!"

The baby merely giggled. The cherubic smile on its chubby face grew sinister and its eyes suddenly burned with malice. Then, slowly, the infant's flesh began to blacken and flake away. A breeze carried the charred skin skyward and fine ashes filled Jay's eyes, threatening to blind him. Through his tears, the boy saw that the baby's flesh was gone and only a sooty skeleton remained.

"Oh, God... oh, God!" cried Jay out loud. He tried to pull his hand away, but the baby's fingers—now thorny black claws of bone—anchored deeply into the meat of his index finger. A numbing coldness began to travel across Jay's knuckles, up his wrist, extending clear to the joint of his elbow.

The baby skeleton in the pit giggled and cooed, the toothless plates of its jaws gnashing and grinding. Of its original, deceptive state only one feature remained. The tiny eyes, blue and livid, remained in the burnt-out eye sockets, shifting and rolling... enjoying Jay's distress.

Finally, Jay broke free of the baby's hold. Instantly, the giggling stopped. In disappointment, the infant began to cry loudly. The tiny bones of its charred hands reached out for Jay, attempting to grab hold of him again.

But the boy had suffered enough of the thing's awful affection. He scrambled backward on his hands and feet, taking the flashlight with him.

Suddenly, a new swath of light spread across the back yard. Jay looked over to see that the back porch light had snapped on. Its hundred-watt bulb shown brightly as someone opened the screen door with a creak of rusty hinges. "Who's out there?" demanded a coarse voice with a thick German accent. It was Old Man Pelingrad. "Whoever it is, show yourself!"

Sluggishly, feeling disoriented and half frozen, Jay pulled himself over the edge of the burning pit and hobbled across the dark yard toward the woods. He kept away from the light of the porch, sticking to the shadows, hoping to reach the thicket unseen.

"Go on now!" yelled Pelingrad angrily. "Get the hell off my property! And don't come back!"

Jay crashed into the woods, groping blindly, careening off the trunks of a couple of trees. He rubbed at his right arm, but it hung frozen and deadened at his side, useless. He misjudged where the dip of the hollow began and abruptly found himself falling. He tumbled, head over heels, down the bank until he landed in a patch of blackberry bramble at the bottom. The thorns pulled at his skin and clothing, snagging, refusing to let go. For one terrifying moment, Jay imagined an entire nursery of fire-blackened baby skeletons clutching at him in the darkness.

Finally, and with some effort, he liberated himself from the briars of the bramble. Then, breathing heavily and scared plumb out of his wits, he began to run in the direction of home.

Behind him echoed the baby in the pit. Its crying had ceased and giggles of amusement rang through the black of night once again.

The following morning found Jay back at the Pelingrad place… but with reinforcements this time.

They stood on the edge of the burning pit: Jay, his father, and Sheriff Sam Biggs. On the other side of the pit, looking frail and harmless, but irritated to no end, was Viktor Pelingrad.

Sheriff Biggs stepped down into the pit and kicked at the ashy dregs, dislodging a blackened Coke bottle. "And you said it was right about here?" asked the lawman.

"Yes, sir," replied Jay softly, staring at his feet. His father stood behind him, his big hands resting on his shoulders, a little too heavily.

"And what was it that you thought you saw, young man?" snapped Pelingrad. His wrinkled face was gaunt and had a hawkish look to it with its long, hooked nose and tiny dark eyes behind thick spectacles. "A… a baby?"

Jay simply nodded. Looking down into the burning pit in broad daylight made his accusation seem stupid and childish.

Pelingrad laughed harshly. "Why, that is pure nonsense, Sheriff!"

"Bullshit is what it is," whispered Cal Abernathy beneath his breath.

Sheriff Biggs looked over at the boy. "Jay, I don't see any evidence of what you've claimed to be true. Is this some sort of prank?"

"No, sir!" piped Jay. "That's the God's honest truth!"

"What was he doing on my property in the first place?" Old Man Pelingrad wanted to know. "Lurking around in the night? He was trespassing, that's what he was doing!"

Biggs walked the perimeter of the pit again, searching the crusty floor, but finding absolutely nothing. "Could it have been a doll, Jay? You know... an old rubber baby doll or something like that?"

"It was a *real* baby!" declared Jay, feeling foolish as he said it. "Or something *like* a baby. I swear it had me by the finger. See?" He held up his right index finger. Thin scratches ran along the flesh, red and inflamed.

"Hush, Jay," said Cal gruffly.

"But, Dad..."

His dad's fingertips bore painfully into the muscles of his shoulders for emphasis. "I said *hush*."

With a sigh, the sheriff stepped up out of the pit. "Well, now, Jay... there's nothing I can do if there's nothing here to do anything about."

"We're sorry we bothered you, Mr. Pelingrad," said Cal Abernathy. "You know boys. Sometimes their imaginations run away with them."

Viktor Pelingrad shook his balding head, disgusted. "I suppose so. But keep him away from my property from now on. Do you understand?"

"Yes, sir," promised Cal. "Come on, Jay."

"But, Dad..." Jay began to protest.

"I said *let's go!*" Roughly, he steered his son toward the driveway and the Abernathys' Dodge Ram pickup.

Sheriff Biggs took another long look at the burning pit before following them. "You be careful with your burning, Mr.

Pelingrad. We don't want it getting out of hand and getting Joe Masterson and the boys down at the fire hall all worked up, do we?"

Pelingrad glared at the constable. "Just keep that damned boy away from my place," was all that he said.

As Jay and Cal were climbing into the pickup, Biggs looked the coach in the eyes. "Keep a handle on your boy, Cal. I don't want to have to come out here again for no reason."

"You got it, Sam," said Cal before slamming the door shut.

Jay sat in the truck next to his father and waited for him to start the engine. Cal didn't. He waited until the sheriff had backed his patrol car onto the highway and headed for town. Then he turned and slapped Jay sharply across the left cheek.

The boy was shocked. His father had spanked him before, but had never stuck him like this. He sat there, addled, for a long moment, the sting of the coach's handprint burning upon his flesh.

"What are you trying to do, boy?" Cal grated angrily. "Are you trying to ruin my reputation? Make me the laughingstock of the county?" His face loomed next to Jay's, huge and red with rage. "Hey, there goes Cal Abernathy and his crazy turd of a boy! Is that what you want, Jay? Hell, I'm a big guy in the community... a football coach. Folks look up to me. I don't need this kind of shit!"

Jay knew he should've kept his mouth shut, but he didn't. "But, I saw it, Dad —"

Cal reached out and grasped Jay's chin roughly between his huge fingers. "Shut up! Just shut the hell up! I don't want to hear this crazy imagination shit of yours... you hear? Holed up in your room with those stupid horror books of yours, rotting your brains when you should be out playing football and stuff like normal boys." His father flung him to the side so violently that his shoulder hit the passenger door hard. "Dammit! I don't know what I did wrong, ending up with a pussy son like you."

Jay tried not to, but he began to cry. His father's words hurt... more than any he'd ever heard before.

Cal Abernathy started up the Ram. "And don't you dare tell your mother about our little conversation," he gritted between clenched teeth. "Or that I hit you like that. If you do, there's plenty more where that came from."

Jay simply sat there, tears coursing down his cheeks as he turned his face to the window.

"Do you understand me?"

"Yes, sir," Jay said bitterly.

Cal put the truck into reverse and began backing down the driveway. "Now dry it up. We're going home."

As they pulled onto the main road, Jay's fear hardened into resentment. He had always known his father was an asshole… but not a dangerous one.

He tried. He really made an effort to do the right thing. But, in the end, it simply didn't take.

For two weeks, Jay resisted the temptation to return to the pit out back of Old Man Pelingrad's house. The night he had encountered the dead baby—or whatever it had been—was always foremost in his mind… and in his nightmares. There was simply no escaping what had happened. What had *really* happened, despite what everyone thought.

Also, the humiliation he had suffered at the hands of his father hadn't done the job Cal Abernathy hoped it would. Jay hadn't "reformed" and miraculously changed into a new son, interested in sports and the things "normal" boys his age were crazy about. If anything, he had grown more introverted and withdrawn, spending all his free time cooped up in his bedroom, the blinds drawn, staring into the gloom. He hadn't even escaped into the comic books and novels he loved so much. Thoughts of the puppy and the baby, the years 1939 and 1946, occupying his mind, turning into an unhealthy obsession.

He began seeing things around the house that disturbed him, things he had never noticed before. How his mother and father didn't talk very much, except on a very basic level. How strange bruises showed up on Mom's arms every so often… oval bruises shaped like large fingerprints. How his mother's face tightened and her eyes dropped sadly when Dad's cell phone rang and he took the call in another room, out of earshot.

Finally, he'd had enough. Jay found that he couldn't wallow

in depression and uncertainty any longer.

It was Halloween night. Jay left his bedroom dressed as Count Dracula, The dead white face, black cape, and streams of fake vampire blood trickling down the corners of his mouth would make him blend with all the other trick-or-treaters that night. His father was out bowling with his league. His mother was watching TV as usual, completely absorbed and oblivious to her surroundings. Jay had always found that to be odd, but now he thought he understood.

He took the flashlight from the utility drawer and ducked out into the night. He didn't go by way of the woods this time. Jay steered his ten-speed down Sycamore Lane, southwestward to where it joined Highway 70. Twenty minutes later, he was braking to a halt a few hundred feet from Viktor Pelingrad's property.

Jay stashed his bike in a drainage ditch, out of sight, then climbed over a split-rail fence into the pasture that stretched to the right side of the Pelingrad property. There was a full moon out that night and it wasn't very hard to see where he was going. It didn't provide much concealment from prying eyes, either. Jay crouched low to the high weeds, keeping a lookout for Old Man Pelingrad. The window of the front parlor blazed like an orange square against the black structure of the house, and he heard the muffled mumble of a television inside. Jay wondered if the old man was watching the same program his mother was.

It wasn't long before he was climbing over the fence at the opposite end. He crept through the woods and came out at the burning pit. The gray ash shone in the moonlight, along with bits of glass and metal that the fire failed to consume. Jay didn't need the flashlight. He set it on the ground, then stepped down into the broad basin of the pit and started toward the calendar that was set firmly in the crust of the charred garbage.

As he walked, that terrible, numbing cold traveled up his feet into his legs. He looked down to see frost coating the laces of his sneakers and the denim of his jeans. Jay didn't consider retreating, though. He continued toward the calendar and the very center of Pelingrad's pit.

By the time he reached the spot, the date on the calendar

had changed five times. The numbers had melted and reformed in rapid succession. Finally, it stopped on 1956. Jay looked for the newspaper and found it. The headline read PRESIDENT EISENHOWER APPROVES INTERSTATE ROADWAY BILL. What was hidden beneath it this time was scarcely concealed at all. Jay hesitated, his heart pounding and his mind swimming dizzily. Then he continued forward.

This time it was not one form trapped in the crust of the fire pit, but *two.* Two trick-or-treaters… one a boy dressed in a sooty black T-shirt and charred Frankenstein mask, the other a ballerina, her pink tutu blackened from flame and her silvery tiara sparkling in the soft glow of the moonlight. Both looked to be around five years old.

The boy looked up at him. Frightened eyes shown through the eyeholes of his monster mask. "Someone stole my candy," he whimpered. "Can you help me find my candy?"

The girl shivered in the cool night. Tears glistened in her tiny blue eyes, matching the fake diamonds in her tiara. "I'm c-c-cold," she sniffled. She reached out with grimy fingers and clutched the tail of Jay's Dracula cape. "I want my mommy!"

"No," whispered Jay. His throat was dry with fear. He felt like he was going crazy. "Leave… leave me alone."

Then, suddenly, the two forms *shifted…* seeming to merge into one. The little girl's clinging grasp grew stronger, more desperate. Jay looked down to find the body of a naked woman, half buried in the hard crust of the fire pit. Her hair was golden blonde and her face was plain, but strong, resembling European women he had seen in photographs before. Her wrists were bound in that rusty bailing wire Jay was accustomed to seeing. The woman's throat had been slit open and ugly stab wounds marred her shoulders, chest, and belly.

Her glassy eyes captured his own and her pale hands clutched the length of black fabric that was tied around his neck. This time Jay didn't attempt to get away. He wanted to know exactly what was going on in this hellish pit of ash and death, and he was certain out of all the apparitions he had witnessed, she alone could tell him the truth.

"Get out of here!" she warned him in the same German

accent that Victor Pelingrad possessed. "Run and never come back again." Tears as black as soot trickled down her high-boned cheeks. "Please, young man, do as I ask."

Jay stared into her face and immediately knew who she was. "Lucinda," he said softly.

Agony shown in the woman's face. "Yes… but you must hurry. There is evil near. It listens to us now… it hears the beating of your heart… smells the sweat of fear upon your flesh. Can you not sense it?"

The boy felt the ashen crust shift under his feet and heard a coarse noise, sort of like the rough hide of a snake rubbing against the bark of a tree. The coldness increased even more than before, radiating up from the pit in frigid waves.

"What evil?" Jay asked. His breath billowed from his mouth in a frosty vapor.

"I am not certain of its origin, only that it is older even than the earth itself," she said softly, urgently. "Satan fears it and God Almighty despises its very existence. Oh, it is horrid, so horrid… and eternally hungry."

"But how did it get here?"

The woman's eyes were bright with fear. "The elder Pelingrad brought it here with him from the Old Country. His intentions were honorable, though. He knew if Hitler ever gained possession of the demon… oh what havoc the madman could have wrought upon this earth!"

"What do you mean?" asked Jay.

"The thing beneath us… it grows more powerful with each life it consumes. It is weak now, but just imagine…" She sobbed, the dark tears running down her face in ebony rivulets. "What if the crematoriums of Auschwitz and Treblinka had not consumed the bodies of twelve million Jews and Gypsies, the lame and the mentally infirmed? What if, instead, the beast had ingested them?" She shuddered violently at the very thought. "The power and devastation! Nothing could have survived its murderous wake!"

Jay was about to ask another question, when the floor of the pit heaved upward, throwing him off balance. The crust of hardened ash split open with a loud, crackling pop and a fiery recess was revealed underneath—a crystal-blue fire born out of coldness and death rather than of heat. A horrid stench assaulted Jay's nostrils. It smelled of brimstone, feces, and putrid decay.

As he stumbled backward, Lucinda's fingers lost their hold. Screaming, she was dragged downward into the widening gap. Jay stared, bewildered into a place much worse than any Hell he had been taught about in Sunday school. A slimy gray monstrosity peppered with infection, boils, and weeping sores writhed sluggishly underneath him. Within its rippling mass floated dozens of its helpless victims... dead, but in some horrible way still alive. Dogs, cats, stray rabbits and squirrels, even a young calf. And then there were those who had been cast there by the Pelingrad family, first by Eric and, later, his son, Viktor. Jay spotted the baby in the cloth diaper, along with the two trick-or-treaters who had been abducted and sacrificed to the demon beneath the backyard burning pit. There were others too, men and women... all damned by the hand of Viktor Pelingrad and his stubborn loyalty to a fiend that had been carried, concealed, in a steamer trunk by ship to American soil.

Jay looked down at them all, forever mired within the thing like helpless creatures trapped in a primeval tar pit, moaning and wailing, tormented in the knowledge that escape would never present itself. At that moment, the horror of what he was looking at struck him and his fascination changed into terror. He turned and leapt out of the pit...

Squarely into the grasp of Viktor Pelingrad.

"So you didn't heed my warning!" he said. "You just had to come back and find out the truth about the pit that my father fashioned." The old man brandished a carving knife, bringing the point beneath Jay's chin, drawing blood. "Well, if you're so confounded anxious to see the beast, then let me introduce you." Roughly, he dragged the boy to edge of the fire pit and tightened his hold on the haft of the knife.

The old man was incredibly stout for his age. No matter how much Jay struggled, Pelingrad's hold remained firm. "It is old and feeble," Viktor told him. "Too feeble to fend for itself. It would perish, if not for the devotion of the Pelingrads."

"Let me go!" screamed Jay. He kicked and thrashed, but

could not escape Viktor's stubborn grasp.

"I'll release you… as soon as blood is let," Pelingrad leered hatefully. "Then your meddlesome soul will remain here always. But you won't be lonely." He laughed softly, his eyes gleaming madly in the darkness. "No, you'll have plenty of company to pass an eternity with."

When Viktor pulled the blade from Jay's throat, placing it just below his breastbone, the boy knew that he had to do something. He entwined his feet with the elderly man's ankles, tripping him up.

Old Man Pelingrad cried out as he lost his balance, lurching forward toward the gaping maw at the bottom of the pit. As he went, he lost his hold on Jay. He was skewered by his own knife as he rolled across the crusty floor and into the putrid pool that seethed underneath.

Viktor screamed, flailing, attempting to pull free, but to struggle was futile. Even as the beast he had cared for consumed him, he could not betray it. "Don't allow it to perish, boy!" he yelled as the crust of the pit began to close over, sealing the abomination from view. "Promise that you shall care for it as I have all these years. You are like me… I know you are. Much more than you care to realize."

Then the earth healed itself and the night grew quiet again. An oppressive silence pressed against Jay's eardrums for a long moment, then the crickets regained their nerve and began their chirring chorus once again.

Feeling exhausted and cold, Jay didn't bother crossing the pasture, but walked up the driveway instead. As he pulled his bike from the ditch and began the tiresome journey home, he thought of Viktor Pelingrad's final words, full of urgency and accusation. *You are like me. Much more than you care to realize.*

Jay tried to dismiss the words, tried to deny the ugly truth that they held. But they stayed with him, refusing to fade. They sank into him, became a part of him, like those poor souls who had forever become a part of the beast beneath Pelingrad's pit.

Several months passed. Fall passed into winter and winter into the spring of a new year.

Jay did his best to avoid the highway that stretched in front of Viktor Pelingrad's abandoned farmhouse. But sometimes when out riding his bike, he would stop and survey the pit from the safety of the driveway. Even at that distance he could sense the thing's anguish. Its hunger drifted across the Pelingrad property in cold waves until ice began to form on the ten-speed's handlebars and Jay was forced to leave. The beast was lonesome and frightened. With no one there to feed it, it was slowly starving to death.

In a way, Jay found himself almost feeling sorry for it. But then again, that could be the monster using some sort of psychic trickery to cause him to react in such a way. *Forget about the thing and let it die,* he told himself. *It sure didn't show its victims any mercy.*

But, afterward, he would always end up regretting those thoughts. He would recall Viktor Pelingrad's frantic words, calling for him to take over its care and protection. And no matter how crazy it sounded, Jay found himself considering the passing of the sword very seriously. *You are like me,* the old man's voice would proclaim, over and over again.

Then came the morning that Jay went down to breakfast to find his mother's throat tattooed with those ugly oval bruises and her eyes moist and red from crying most of the night. Later he found his father's suitcase packed in the floor of his bedroom closet and a pair of tickets to Bermuda lying openly on his nightstand, without shame. That night the phone calls came more frequently. His father neglected to duck into the other room this time. He talked in flirty tones, outlining clandestine plans, staring straight at Jay's mother and smirking all the while.

It infuriated Jay, but there was nothing he could do.

Or was there?

The following afternoon found Jay Abernathy back at the Pelingrad property. Not lingering hesitantly in the driveway this time… but sitting within the ashen circle of the old fire pit.

He had left a note on the windshield of his father's pickup truck, tucked beneath the windshield wiper. A note that was going to push all the right buttons.

Jay sat there, feeling the cold radiate up from the earth beneath him, even relishing it. It seemed to harden something with him…freezing his heart, but turning everything else as crystal clear as ice. And he couldn't deny that it felt pretty damned good.

He heard the roar of an engine, the crackle of gravel, the angry slamming of a truck door. "Jay! Where the hell are you?"

The layer of crusty ash beneath him shuddered slightly and buckled.

The boy patted the ground beneath him. "Just be patient," he whispered soothingly. "Here he comes."

Jay knew that what he was doing was wrong. That it might even be a sin in the eyes of God.

But one little snack wouldn't hurt… now would it?

RK

Mister Mack & the Monster Mobile

"Come on, will you?" called Jimmy. "Get the lead outta your butt!"

Kyle Sadler pumped the pedals of his bike, trying desperately to catch up. "What's the big hurry?"

"He said he had to hit road by three. It's past one-thirty right now."

Kyle grumbled to himself as they left the busy stretch of Fesslers Lane and headed into the industrial park. Sometimes his best friend, Jimmy Jackson, drove him crazy, especially when he got some stupid idea stuck in his head.

"Watch out for trucks!" he warned the boy ahead of him. "You don't want to get run over, do you?" The industrial park was usually swarming with tractor trailers.

Jimmy looked over his shoulder and rolled his eyes. "It's the Sunday before Halloween. Nobody's working today, remember?"

Kyle decided to keep his mouth shut. There was no reasoning with Jimmy when he was like this. Together, they sped beneath an interstate overpass. Above, cars and trucks roared on their way through East Nashville.

A minute later, they were there. They coasted into a vacant lot choked with weeds and crushed gravel. A couple of factories stood to the right and left, but like Jimmy said, it was Sunday. They were completely deserted.

"Great! He's still here," said Jimmy with relief.

Kyle looked at the big travel camper parked in the middle of the abandoned lot. It was one of those expensive kinds, like the country music stars parked on Music Row downtown. It was black and gray, its windows tinted so dark that you couldn't see through them. There were a few Halloween cling-ems stuck here and there: a skeleton, a witch, a black cat.

"I'm not sure about this, Jimmy," he said after they parked their bikes a few yards away.

Jimmy did that eye-rolling thing again, making Kyle want to punch him right good. "The old man's okay, I tell you. He's kind of like my grandpa, but a lot cooler. It's not like he's some kinda pediaphobe or something."

"That's pedophile, gerbil-brain," Kyle told him. "Why is he parked out here in the middle of nowhere?"

Jimmy glared at him, irritated by his bellyaching. "Hey, I only brought you out here because you're so crazy about the stuff. I mean, we can head back to the house and sit around bored out of our skulls, if you want."

"No. No, that's okay. Just seems awful weird, him being out here, that's all."

Jimmy hopped off his bike and knocked on the bus door. They stood in the cool October breeze for a long, expectant moment. Then the door opened with a pneumatic *whoosh*.

Kyle studied the man who stood there. He was in his mid-seventies, a little heavy, with thinning hair and a white beard. He wore a black Hawaiian shirt decorated with leering orange jack-o'-lanterns, khaki pants, and gray Crocs. Behind his eyeglasses were kind eyes, sparkling with a youthfulness that his face had lost long ago.

"Hi, boys," he greeted. "Glad to see you. I was afraid you couldn't make it."

"I had a little trouble convincing Kyle to come," Jimmy told him. "Get this… he thinks you might be some kinda child molester or something."

The man smiled warmly and regarded Kyle. "Smart boy. Sounds like he has a good head on his shoulders. But, hey, I'm just a retired fella, seeing the country, that's all. You have nothing to fear from me, son." He reached out and shook the boy's hand. "You can just call me Mr. Mack."

"See?" said Jimmy. "I told you he was okay."

Kyle felt his anxiety drop a notch or two. "Jimmy said you had some cool stuff in your bus."

Mr. Mack's eyes twinkled. "I do... if you like horror movies."

"Kyle lives on that stuff." He turned to the boy next to him. "Don't you?"

Kyle simply nodded. Despite his apprehension, he felt excited; anxious to see the treasures that Jimmy claimed was inside.

The elderly man stepped to the side and motioned into the bus. "Then, please, enter the Monster Mobile."

Together, the boys climbed the steep stairs into the cab of the camper. The moment they reached the top of the steps, the doors shut behind them, sealing out the sun and the distant roar of the interstate.

Kyle felt that squirming ball of nerves in the pit of his stomach again. If his mom knew he was doing this, she would pitch a major fit.

"Right through there, boys," said Mr. Mack. "Take your time. There's a lot to see."

They turned toward a black velvet curtain that separated the cab from the rest of the camper. "Come on," said Jimmy with a big grin on his freckled face. "You're gonna love this!"

Kyle swallowed dryly. "Okay."

Then they stepped through the dark curtains.

The overhead lights of the camper's interior were dim, so, at first, Kyle had a hard time seeing exactly what was there. He expected to see outside through the tinted windows, but it was as though they weren't even there. Instead, the walls of the camper were covered with a vast collection of movie memorabilia and exhibits. The kind of stuff that Kyle's bedroom was decorated with... except this was the real deal.

Vintage movie posters of *Bride of Frankenstein* and *King Kong* lined the walls, along with framed photos of some of Hollywood's greatest horror actors standing beside a younger version of Mr. Mack. Legends like Boris Karloff, Lon Chaney, Jr., and Vincent Price. And each photograph was personally autographed to their gracious host.

Along the length of the camper stood rows of glass cases displaying some very recognizable movie props. The silver wolf's head cane from *The Wolfman*, the Monster's woolen vest and stacked shoes from *Son of Frankenstein,* one of Ray Harryhausen's stop-motion models from *Jason and the Argonauts,* a little worse for wear, but still intact. There were dozens of other props, too, all from some of Kyle's favorite monster movies.

Amazed, he walked over to a case that held a face mask and hands from *The Creature from the Black Lagoon.* "Is this stuff for real?"

Mr. Mack chuckled and nodded. "Everything here is genuine. I have the documentation to prove it. That's one of the original masks that Ricou Browning wore during his swimming sequences as the Gillman. See that tiny port on the crown of the head? That's where the bubbles escaped from the diving apparatus he wore beneath the suit."

"Isn't this great?" asked Jimmy. He was peering into a case bearing Leatherface's patchwork mask and chainsaw from *The Texas Chainsaw Massacre.*

"How did you get your hands on of all this?" Kyle asked.

Mr. Mack's eyes gleamed. "Do I detect a hint of skepticism? Well, years ago, I used to be a makeup artist in Hollywood. You know, latex appliances and stuff like that. I learned my craft from some of the best in the business, including Jack Pierce. I retired in the early Seventies and took my collection of memorabilia on the road. I reckon I just couldn't bear the thought of this stuff being stuck in some musty old museum. I'd rather take it to the public, so fans can enjoy it."

Kyle moved to the next case. He stared at the object hanging in its temperature-controlled case. "What's this?"

"That's the original cape from the movie *Dracula,*" said Mr. Mack.

Kyle eyed the man suspiciously. "I thought Bela Lugosi was buried in his Dracula cape."

The old man smiled. "That's just an urban legend. Bela gave me that cape a day or two before he died." He pointed to a framed photo over the case that showed a decrepit Lugosi handing the vampire cape to Mr. Mack.

"I was certain that he was buried in it," said Kyle beneath his breath. Despite all the wonders around him, the boy was beginning to think that the illustrious Mr. Mack was a downright fake. Kyle had read everything he could get his hands on concerning the old Universal monster movies and their actors. And there was one thing he knew for sure… Bela Lugosi *was* laid to rest in his Dracula cape. That was fact, not rumor.

"So you're retired?" asked Jimmy. He marveled at the gray wig, flower-print dress, and butcher knife that Anthony Perkins had made famous in Hitchcock's *Psycho*. "You don't work on any of this stuff anymore?"

"Oh, I dabble in it from time to time," admitted Mr. Mack. "It's hard to stop once you get it in your blood, I suppose."

Kyle suddenly felt claustrophobic in the dark confines of the belly of the bus. "Well, I think we'd better get going," he said.

Jimmy looked at him incredulously. "Are you kidding? You haven't even checked out half of these exhibits yet. Why do you want to leave?"

"I promised Dad that I'd help him rake the leaves this afternoon," Kyle told him firmly.

"Sorry that you've gotta run so soon," said Mr. Mack regretfully. "But before you go, let me show you something that I've been fiddling with in my workshop." He started toward another black velvet partition at the back of the bus. "Just stay right here. I'll be right back. You're gonna love this!"

When he had disappeared through the dark curtain, Jimmy turned to his friend. "What's the deal? I bring you out here to meet this guy because you love this monster stuff so much and you want to cut out right in the middle of it? I thought you'd have a million questions for the guy… about all those great monster movies and the ones who acted in them."

"This guy is a big fake," Kyle whispered, not wanted the old man to overhear their conversation. "I don't think he worked with any of them. And I think he's lying about being a makeup artist. I've read tons of books on the subject and never once came across anyone named Mack."

"But what about all these cool props? They're for real, aren't they?"

"I doubt it," said Kyle. "Oh, they're elaborate fakes, but I don't think they're the real props. And those photos of him and

Karloff and Lugosi… well, you can trick up any kind of photo with a computer these days."

Jimmy shook his head in disgust. "Okay, okay! We'll go. But, if you ask me, you're just being paranoid."

Abruptly the rustle of curtains drew their attention. They turned and gasped.

Behind them, dressed in the black-and-orange Hawaiian shirt and khakis, was a hideous monster.

At least his head was that of some horrid creature. The tanned arms and legs were still those of their elderly host, Mr. Mack. Kyle stared, startled, at the monster's face. The skin was a glossy charcoal gray in color with knotty black veins running throughout, like the exposed roots of a tree. The eyes were bulbous and moist, yellow with a network of bulging purple veins and shiny green pupils. It was the teeth that caused his heart to race the most, though. They were small and black, but wickedly jagged and as sharp as razor blades.

Kyle had seen hundreds of horror movies, but never had he seen a creature that looked so damned *real*.

"Man, you gave us a start!" said Jimmy, finally catching his breath. "That mask just about made me crap in my britches!"

Mr. Mack chuckled. It came out as a soft, wet, bubbling noise.

Slowly, Kyle began to back toward the front of the bus.

"Don't tell me that you're still spooked!" laughed Jimmy. He turned back to the man in the Hawaiian shirt. "Great mask, Mr. Mack. But how did you make it? You haven't lost your touch. I really like how you make the veins throb like that."

Mr. Mack said nothing. He simply started forward… grinning…. with those jagged, black teeth.

"Let's get out of here!" urged Kyle. He suddenly smelled a strange odor in the air of the bus. A stench sort of like the marigolds his mother had planted this past summer.

"What?" Jimmy seemed disoriented, as he stared at his pal. "What's that terrible stink?"

"It's coming from *him*!" Kyle wondered if he should have said *it*.

Jimmy began to follow his friend, but his face grew strangely pale and he began to gasp for breath. "I… I don't feel right," he said. "My legs…" He collapsed under his own weight. "They… they aren't working."

Kyle tried his best to reach the curtained partition at the front of the bus, but he too was beginning to feel weak and out of kilter. His nasal passages began to sting and his tongue grew numb. "What's happening?" he muttered thickly, then fell into the aisle between the display cases. His arms and legs began to twitch and convulse involuntarily.

Mr. Mack started toward them, tiny teeth grating one against the other.

"Oh, God," whimpered Jimmy, unable to move now. "He *is* a pediaphobe."

"Pedophile," corrected Kyle sadly. His voice was barely audible, even to himself.

The boy lay on his back staring at the recessed lighting of the ceiling. Then there he was. Mr. Mack… or what masqueraded as Mr. Mack. He stared at Kyle for a long moment with those bulging yellow eyes. Then he bent downward and, with no effort at all, lifted Kyle into his arms.

"No," whispered Kyle. "Please."

"Don't worry," he was assured in that wet, guttural voice that had replaced the elderly man's kindly tone. "I won't hurt you. I promise."

Mr. Mack turned and, almost tenderly, began to carry him toward the chamber at the back of the bus.

As Kyle's consciousness began to fade, panic suddenly spiked in the ten-year-old's brain. *What's he going to do to me?* his thoughts screamed. *Rape me? Kill me?* He stared up at those sharp little teeth, gnashing in festered gray gums. *Eat me?*

With the last, lingering bit of energy he could muster, he reached out with his right hand and clawed at the man's left arm. The skin with its liver spots and coarse white hair came away in his hand. Latex. Underneath was the same wet, gray flesh that covered the face that leered horribly down at him.

"Don't be afraid," said Mr. Mack soothingly. "Trust me."

Then Kyle was carried through the folds of the black curtains and into a much deeper darkness.

Phillip Mitchell checked his paperwork and nodded grimly. Then he opened the door to Room 439 and knocked quietly. "Mind if I come in?" he asked.

Betty Sadler looked up from a romance novel she had been reading and smiled. "Hi, Dr. Mitchell."

"How's my favorite patient today?" he asked. He took Kyle's chart from the foot of the bed and checked it. He took a pen from the breast pocket of his white coat and made a few necessary notes.

"He seems less agitated," said the boy's mother. "He's resting better than he did yesterday."

"I suppose he just had to regain his bearings… after what happened," the doctor told her. "So, how are you doing?"

Betty closed her book and shook her head. Tears bloomed in her eyes. "I don't know. Frankly, I'm not sure how to feel. I'm sorry… I'm having a difficult time with this."

Mitchell laid a reassuring hand on her trembling shoulder. "Kyle is going to be okay. You have nothing to worry about."

The woman wiped away her tears, but her fear remained. "Doctor… did that bastard… did he…?" She couldn't bring herself to say the word. "The tests yesterday… the examination?"

Doctor Mitchell crouched down until his face was level with hers. "I'm going to be blunt, Mrs. Sadler, but only for your own peace of mind. No, we found no evidence of sexual abuse. And there was no trace of semen whatsoever."

"Thank God."

"Doc?" came a weak voice from behind them.

Mitchell stood and turned toward the bed. Kyle was awake. He lay there, hooked up to IVs and monitors, looking pale. The flesh around his eyes appeared dark and shadowy, almost bruised.

"Good morning, little buddy," said the doctor. "How are you feeling today?"

"Weaker than water," said the boy with a sigh. "Better than yesterday, I guess."

The physician did a short examination, checking his vital

signs, pupil dilation, and breathing. He laid the flat of his palm on the boy's midsection for a long moment. The boy flinched. "Still tender?"

"A little," admitted Kyle.

Doctor Mitchell sat on the edge of the bed and smiled at the ten-year-old. "I don't want to upset you, Kyle, but someone from the police department will be stopping by later on to talk to you. About what happened in the industrial park."

Kyle shrugged his shoulders weakly. "I don't really remember much of anything. It's all pretty hazy."

The doctor was thoughtful for a moment. "Kyle... could you tell me about the man in the camper? This 'Mr. Mack'? Can you describe him to me?"

A haunted look shown in the boy's sunken eyes. "He just looked like a harmless old man," he told the doctor. "Almost bald, a white beard, glasses." Then Kyle's voice lowered a bit, almost fearfully. "But that wasn't his *real* face."

Abruptly, a crash came from the adjoining bathroom. They turned their eyes to see a middle-aged black woman in green scrubs standing in the doorway. Her eyes were wide. Startled.

"Hi, Sophie," said Mitchell. "I didn't know you were in there."

"I was cleaning," she said.

"Everything okay?"

"Yes, sir. I just dropped something that's all." She stared not at the doctor, but at the boy in the bed. Then she turned and went back to work.

Doctor Mitchell smiled at his patient. "You rest up, Kyle, and I'll check in on you later."

"Okay," agreed Kyle.

The doctor stood up and started toward the door.

"Uh, Doc? How's Jimmy doing?"

Mitchell wondered if his smile looked too forced and false. He hoped not. "We'll talk about Jimmy later." Then he left before the boy could ask any further questions.

As he left the fourth-floor pediatric ward and started back to his office, Doctor Mitchell mulled over Kyle Sadler's condition in his mind. The boy was terribly anemic, his white cell count extremely low. But that wasn't what concerned him. It was the tests that had him worried. Particularly the CAT scan they had done yesterday afternoon.

He hadn't exactly told Betty Sadler the entire truth. Kyle had been abused, but not sexually. Rather, the tests had shown that the boy had been mistreated in other, more subtle ways.

For lack of a better term, Mitchell referred to it as *anatomical molestation.* The natural position of several of Kyle's internal organs had been altered. The boy's liver had swapped places with his stomach, and his kidneys were positioned at the front of his abdominal cavity, rather than the rear. The pancreas was completely missing and, in its place, was a strange organ that shouldn't have even been there… but one that served the exact same function. Mitchell had not done exploratory surgery on the boy, but he knew how the organ looked—pear-shaped and pale purple, almost lavender in color. He also knew that the cellular tissue was unlike any known to man. Living tissue that was totally alien to modern medicine.

He knew that for a fact, because Kyle wasn't the first child to be admitted into his care. Three others, a boy and two girls, had suffered similar fates during the past two months, and all possessed that strange, new organ where their pancreas once was.

Another thing that concerned Mitchell was the matter of Jimmy Jackson. He hadn't told Kyle, but his best friend was missing. When Kyle had been discovered alongside his bike in the vacant lot, he had been found alone.

That evening, as she cleaned the big windows of the hospital lobby, Sophie Taylor stared into the rainy twilight beyond the panes. Her hands trembled nervously as she worked.

"Sophie?"

She turned at the sound of the man's voice and found Phillip Mitchell standing behind her, dressed in his street clothes. At first, she could only stare at him.

"Sophie… are you alright?" he asked, concerned. "You seemed upset this afternoon… in Kyle Sadler's room."

She wanted so badly to tell him, but, instead, she lied. "I'm okay, Dr. Mitchell. It's just this business with the children. It has me spooked, that's all."

The doctor nodded. "I know how you feel."

No, she thought. *You couldn't possibly know.*

"Well, good night, Sophie," said Doctor Mitchell. Then he left the lobby and sprinted through the rain toward his car.

She watched as he pulled out of the parking lot and into the traffic. *You should have told him,* she thought. Absently, she pressed the palm of her hand against her belly, just below the diaphragm and felt the steady *thrum-thrum-thrum* of a pulse where none should have been.

Sophie had taught herself to ignore it, but it had grown stronger since the children were admitted.

It had happened a long time ago, back in Alabama. It was 1974. She had been nine years old. She was walking home from the store when a man pulled up in his camper... a Winnebago, she believed it was. Balding, white beard, eyeglasses. He had been black, though, not white. *But that wasn't his real face,* the boy in Room 439 had said.

He had asked her if she liked monster movies. Of course, she had said yes. She and her sister went to the picture show every Saturday and saw all those spooky movies that came out. After it was over, they found her in a creek bed, nearly dead. Folks thought that she'd had a seizure or something. She never told them about him. She didn't know why. They would have probably thought she was crazy if she had.

Tears formed in Sophie's eyes, but she wiped them away with the back of her hand before anyone could notice. *Lord Jesus, help me,* she prayed. *Please, tell me what to do.*

As she continued her cleaning, she saw a camper pull into the hospital parking lot. Not a Winnebago, but one of those big fine buses... black with gray trim.

An eerie feeling overtook her. *It's probably just some family visiting a patient,* she told herself. Sometimes kinfolk from out of state would show up in campers, to avoid paying for a hotel.

The pulse in her abdomen grew stronger. *Thrum, thrum, thrum.* She nearly doubled over as it began to quicken.

What's the matter with me? she wondered. At first she was

sure that she was having a heart attack. But this had nothing at all to do with her heart.

THRUM, THRUM, THRUM!

The *ding* of the elevator sounded across the lobby behind her and she turned.

Sophie caught a fleeting glimpse of a lab coat, with the trace of a Hawaiian shirt between the lapels. Black with orange Halloween pumpkins.

Then the doors closed and the elevator began to climb steadily toward the fourth floor.

HARVEST
TOMMY
SALLY
JOE

The Halloween Train

"Daddy... is the Halloween Train for real?" asked Donnie.

"No," his father told him. "Not anymore."

But it had been once. His parents had taken him several times, on the train that traveled to the little town of Harvest and a wondrous night of trick-or-treating. Then, when he was Donnie's age, he had missed the festivities due to sickness. It was the year that the train had derailed and 139 children had never made it to Harvest alive.

That night, as All Hallows Eve came to a close, Donnie dreamt that he and Daddy waited beside railroad tracks, broken and long abandoned. He was still dressed in his goblin costume, candy bag in hand. His father sat on a log beside the black forest, sleeping, using a suitcase as a pillow.

From out of the mist it came, slithering like a long, black snake through the night. "Wake up, Daddy," he said. "It's really coming."

Then it was there before them. Dark, silent... waiting.

"All aboard!" called the conductor. "Room for two more."

With Donnie's urging, Daddy sluggishly left the log and they mounted the stairs. Inside sat cowboys, princesses, pirates, and ballerinas. Each of their pale and painted faces was set in a frightening rictus of both horror and delight.

When the train lurched forward on its journey, Daddy's eyes cleared. "Where are we?"

Donnie simply smiled.

Beyond the windows, somewhere in the mist, he could hear Mommy begging... pleading... for them to wake up.

LIFE-LIKE, RUBBER
FRIGHT MASKS

The Candy in the Ditch Gang

At the risk of sounding chauvinistic, I believe that Halloween has always been—and will forever be—a boy's holiday.

Oh, sure, girls are really into it on October 31st. They love the costumes and the candy. But the girls of my era (the mid-'60s and early '70s) were more interested in Frankie Avalon or the Beatles, than Frankenstein, Dracula, or the Wolfman. They had more important things to do than spend their Saturday afternoons putting together Aurora monster models or rushing down to the corner drugstore for the latest issue of *Famous Monsters of Filmland Magazine.* They lacked something that the majority of red-blooded males possessed… an almost limitless fascination with the macabre and an unending desire to be "totally grossed out."

I believe I would be safe in the assumption that a lot of boys between the ages of eight and twelve view the approach of All Hallows Eve with the same reverence that some folks view the Second Coming. I know I did at that age.

The amount of preparation during the four-week period prior to the big night shows the degree of devotion involved. First, there are the decorations. Back in my day, we didn't have fake cobwebs, yard zombies, or life-like bats, rats, and spiders. And we sure didn't have life-sized animatronic witches and monsters who actually talk and, yes, even sing and dance (the mere thought of possessing such a wondrous thing back in the '60s and '70s would have been more than our youthful minds could have handled!). No, we were satisfied with a meticulously carved jack-o'-lantern and a jointed, glow-in-the-dark skeleton we bought at the Ben Franklin five-and-dime in town.

Then there was the selection of precisely "what we would

be" on the important night… alias "our secret Halloween identity." At the ages of three through seven, the pre-packaged costumes in a box were acceptable. Monsters, superheroes, astronauts, and TV stars were the most popular. The brittle plastic masks were cheaply rendered and the full-length body suits of non-flammable material were okay for the unseasoned tyke. I remember in the fall of 1966, the entire boyhood nation was bitten by the Batman bug. That Halloween, the streets were teaming with miniature Batmen (no Robins… who wanted to be that sissy-pants Boy Wonder?). I was a member of that legion of Dark Knights on that dark night, polyester cape flapping, running down sidewalks and leaping upon porches without the aid of a tethered Batarang. Unlike my counterparts, I had talked my mother into cutting off the bottom half of my face mask, leaving only the cowl above. This puzzled my fellow Caped Crusaders to the point of irritation, but while they sweated and struggled for oxygen beneath their unaltered masks, I breathed in the cool, crisp air with great abandon, resembling—in my six-year-old mind, at least—a heroic and debonair Adam West.

As our age progressed, we cast aside the baby costumes and advanced to the next level… the latex rubber monster mask. Oh, how we yearned for those detailed Don Post creations that were offered in the back pages of *Famous Monsters*, but, alas, who our age had $39.95 back then, and an additional $18.95 for the matching hands? So we compromised. On the first day of October, my cousins and I would converge on Grant's Department Store (a precursor to Wal-Mart) and head to their celebrated Halloween section. There, amid everything else, was a huge bin-table that was a good foot deep with every cheap rubber monster mask imaginable. You could find just about anything if you searched long enough… gorillas, devils, zombies, cavemen, werewolves, vampires. Some had hair, some didn't. There could have been a nest of rabid rats holed up in there, but we didn't care. We dug and rooted through that truckload of latex, trying them on, making sure the eyeholes aligned properly. Sure, we'd get a snide comment from a sales lady or the store manager about "spreading germs," but it failed to faze us. We searched for maybe an hour or so, just to find the right one.

Later on, when we had reached the wisdom of double-digit age, we would experiment with costumes other than those that involved masks. White and black greasepaint, rubber scars you stuck to your face, and plenty of fake vampire blood. Occasionally, you wanted to do something completely different from the usual monster fare. One Halloween season I pretty much pestered my mother to death about dressing myself up as the Amazing Colossal Man. But she refused to let me go out in public dressed in nothing but a bald-headed wig and a loincloth.

Then there came the actual night of Halloween itself. That afternoon we usually had a party at school: playing games, getting treat bags from the teacher, and bobbing for apples (talk about spreading germs! Yeeech!) Then, that evening after supper, we'd suit up for battle and go trick-or-treating. Back in the mid-'60s, folks seemed a little more trusting of one another than they do now, and parents especially so of their kids. If the young'uns were really young, a parent would accompany them, but if they were older than seven, they were pretty much set loose like a pack of candy-hungry Tasmanian devils, while their folks stayed home and gave out treats. I remember us wandering all over our small town with a freedom that is no longer possible in today's dangerous world. There weren't that many cars out back then; just gangs of trick-or-treaters on the prowl, with no reflective clothing or flashlights. The darkness was our friend and we embraced it.

And there were always one or two houses that were considered "haunted," either by ghosts or by particularly weird folks... but you still went there, if only for the thrill of bragging that you survived the visit. I remember back in '72, my brother, my cousin, and I went to the house of a new family that had moved into town only a couple of months previous to Halloween. Unlike the usual houses, where our treats were deposited on the doorstep, we were actually invited inside at this one... and, despite our better judgment, we actually took them up on their invitation. "There's someone in the den who would like to see you," said a skinny, bird-like lady. We walked into the room to find an overweight man in a leather recliner, dressed up like an evil clown. He had a wild, multi-colored wig, white face, red rubber nose, and a wicked-looking grin. "Come closer," he beckoned with a bone-chilling giggle. Frightened (but deliciously so!) we crept forward. The guy stank of beer and unfiltered Camels. He deposited a wrapped popcorn ball in our sacks and said "Come back and see me again next year… if you dare!" We left that house feeling like we'd been in the presence of a true monster and that we had survived the encounter. For all we knew, the fellow's wife could have been a bone-gnawing cannibal and he could have been the most vile child molester/ murderer on the face of the earth, but, at that age, we didn't care. It was a Halloween visit that we would remember and talk about for years afterward.

Of course, returning home with that night's booty intact was another story. It was common for us to romp through the darkness, stepping into sinkholes or falling into ditches, ripping our treat bags on tree branches or thorny shrubs. Sometimes we would make it home to find that half our candy was gone, lost somewhere along the way. The next day, after school, we would go out looking for lost treats. It was almost like an Easter egg hunt on the first of November. Bubble gum and Bit-O-Honeys would litter the lawns. If it had rained the night before, you could find bite-sized Babe Ruths bobbing in the drainage ditches like brightly-packaged turds in the bottom of a toilet.

These days, trick-or-treating is a different matter entirely. Parents have almost abandoned the practice of going door-to-door in favor of taking their kids to the local mall or a non-secular party at their local church, where ghosts and goblins, and particularly witches, are frowned upon.

Luckily, my kids still have the opportunity to experience Halloween the way it should be. In the nearby town of Gordonsville, hundreds of trick-or-treaters converge on the town's main street, going from door to door without fear. Everyone knows everyone else there and the town police are out and about to keep order. Folks sit on their porches with big bowls of candy or treat bags, commenting on how cute or creative the kids costumes are, while socializing with the parents. It is a community celebration that is rare in this uncertain day and time and I'm thankful that my children are fortunate enough to take part in it every year.

Sometimes, when I'm standing at the end of the sidewalk, watching my young'uns on the doorstep with their bags extended and the words "Trick-or-Treat!" on their lips, a nostalgic feeling nearly overcomes me. I kind of wish I was a foot or two shorter, dressed in a Creature from the Black Lagoon mask, feeling the satisfying weight of a pound or two of candy in the bottom of my treat bag. Those days are past, but, through my children, I can still relive the magic of those wonderful Halloweens past.

— October 2009

HALLOWEENS: PAST & PRESENT

Halloweens: Past & Present

Well, another Halloween has passed and this one turned out to be a particularly fun and pleasant one. No ill-tempered young'uns, no costume malfunctions, no rushing off to someone's particular house across town to catch them before they turned off the porch light and stashed away the candy bowl. No, this October 31st turned out to be a pretty easygoing one and absolutely perfect weather-wise down here in Middle Tennessee. Cool, blustery, and with a big ol' full moon, to boot. You could almost hear the werewolves howling in delight.

The Kelly kids certainly seemed to have a good time. My oldest daughter, Reilly, dressed up as a purple-haired punk rocker, my five-year-old, Makenna, went as Hanna Montana (surprised?) and my nineteen-month-old son, Ryan, was decked out as Batman. Without the cowl, that is. Ryan's kind of funny about stuff on his face and head. He hates wearing caps and hats, so he certainly wasn't about to please dear old dad and wear his Batman mask. Funny... whenever the girls deck him out in a golden tiara (to my horror!) during playtime, he'll parade around the house wearing the thing for a good half hour. Better trade that dime-store crown for a John Deere cap, my boy... if only for your father's peace of mind.

One thing that made this year's trick-or-treating run smooth as silk is the spread of Trunk-or-Treat in the area. Several of the local churches did it last year. Folks would park in the church parking lot with their trunks open, full of treats and decorations. The kids ate it up (along with the candy) and the social interaction was fun for children and parents alike. This year Trunk-or-Treat went a step further. Several of the town merchants and churches decided to set up on the town square, some with their trunks open, some with booths. The volunteer fire department was even handing out drinks and hot dogs. And of course we visited family, as well.

All in all, a very pleasant and memorable Halloween for the entire Kelly clan.

Of course, not all the Halloweens of my life have been as pleasant and brimming with good memories. One particular Halloween comes hauntingly to mind. One that still leaves an ugly shadow upon my yearly celebration, even across the lengthy span of 42 years.

When I was a kid, I grew up in a picturesque Southern town. It was nestled in a valley surrounded by wooded hills. Railroad tracks ran straight through this lovely hamlet. There were several churches, a grocery store, a post office, and a single elementary school (which, incidentally, was located directly behind my back yard). Kids could ride their bikes from one end of town to the other without worrying about gangs or child molesters. And our Halloweens were the same—full of freedom and frights in the darkness, without our parents following us around in cars.

But my town wasn't a perfect town. Far from it. It possessed its share of bigotry and racial injustice. To the north stood a tall hill where all the black folks in town lived. It was known by all as N——r Hill (I'm sure you can fill in the blanks if you use a little imagination). The town dump was on that hill, along with tin and tarpaper shacks that no one should have been condemned to live in. But, unfortunately, it was merely a fact of life back then. My journeys to the town dump were always a sad sojourn, witnessing unfortunate poverty from within the safety of my father's two-toned '56 Chevy. Compounding my misery was my father's constant barrage of comments and n——r jokes. I loved my father dearly, but he was raised as many were in that era, with an air of racial superiority and little tact to go with it. I can recall feeling a mixture of anger, sadness, and fear, wondering if he would go to hell for his constant use (and abuse) of the N-word.

Thus, the Halloween of my eighth year comes uncomfortably to mind. It was 1968 and it was a dark and dangerous time in my home town. During the April of that year, Martin Luther King had been assassinated at the Lorraine Motel in Memphis and, in turn, people we had never seen as much of a threat now seemed to possess the potential to be so. I remember hearing my elders talk about how "uppity" the black folks were getting following the death of Doctor King and how something ugly was liable to happen, due to anger and bad feelings between the occupants of N---gr Hill and the townsfolk below. Animosity between the races was building at a steady pace and it seemed like only a matter of time before hostile feelings got the better of reason, in both whites and blacks.

That Halloween night had a different feeling to it. There was a blanket of tension over the entire community, and particularly in the faces of my mother and father. My parents forbid us to stray beyond the stretch of our street, but wouldn't give us a concrete explanation why that restriction had been set. Still, we netted a bagful of Halloween candy by eight o'clock. As was customary, my brother, Kevin, and I would don our pajamas by eight-thirty and begin the task of separating our treasure trove of candy into separate piles: bubble gum, suckers, candy bars, etc.

It was nearing nine o'clock, when the worst fears of my hometown almost came true… within our own house.

Someone knocked on our door and, being the trusting lady she was, my mother went to answer it. As I arranged my candy, I heard her say "What do you want?" and then, in growing alarm, "You can't come in here!" I turned and looked through the door that lay between the living room and the combination kitchen and den. There were six or seven tall young black men entering the house, silently, but deliberately. They said nothing at all. They simply walked in, carrying the smell of autumn wood smoke and damp leaves with them. I recall my mother backing into the den, her face full of fear. There was a strange look in the eyes of those home invaders. I was too young to comprehend that expression at such an early age, but now I would identify it instantly as a mixture of malice and lust.

Two of them were actually through the doorway and in the den, when my father's voice boomed from the end of the hallway near the bathroom. "What are you doing here?" That was when the invaders lost their resolve. They scrambled for the door, afraid that my father was about to shoot at them (which was impossible, since my mother forbid firearms in our home). I remember the last one—a boy no more than fourteen or fifteen years of age—turning and looking at me full in the face. There was as much fear in his eyes as there was in mine. They seemed to say "What the hell am I doing here?" But, before leaving, he couldn't resist grabbing up a handful of my very best candy: Babe Ruths, Butterfingers, and Tootsie Rolls. Then he was out in the darkness and running with the others.

I remember my mother sitting on the couch, her face pale with shock and fear, while my father stood in the yard ranting and raving. I also remember feeling anger at the theft of my candy bars. My brother, only four at the time, didn't seem to realize the potential danger we had been in that night.

Many Halloweens have passed since then and now I can look back at 1968 objectively, with neither anger nor fear, but with understanding. At the age of eight, I knew nothing of the impact Martin Luther King had made upon the African-American community or the anger and loss they had experienced following his brutal killing. But at the age of fifty, I can understand what they might have felt that year, when a smirking white face may have looked hauntingly like James Earl Ray to them and stirred feelings they wouldn't have normally even considered or acted upon.

And, as for my stolen candy, I can't honestly begrudge that frightened teenager his clutching handful of Snickers and Bit-O-Honeys. I figure it may have been well-deserved, considering that he was restricted from trick-or-treating in my neck of the woods; barred from my picturesque Southern street by long-standing prejudice and underlying fear.

Yes, that was a long, long time ago. But when the clock strikes nine on Halloween night, I can't help but think about that knock on our door and the misguided retribution it might have brought.

— November 2010

GLOWS IN THE DARK
AURORA

Monsters in a Box

With it being the Halloween season and all, I can't help but have monsters on the brain lately. We had already decorated most of the house (the living room looks like a chamber of horrors!) but there seemed to be something missing.

"Why don't you put out those old monster models of yours?" one of my daughters suggested.

So I did just that. I opened our old cedar chest (an heirloom passed down by my late mother) and there, nestled between stacks of books, stood my small platoon of surviving monsters... a little dusty, but still intact and ready for display. Most of the Universal Monsters that I loved so much as a child were there: Frankenstein, Dracula, the Wolfman, the Phantom of the Opera, The Mummy, King Kong, and my all-time favorite, the Creature from the Black Lagoon.

I had possessed them all at one time or another, but, sadly, some had become damaged and were discarded along the way. Just bringing these out of storage and sprucing them up for Halloween brought back cherished memories of those days when I was nine or ten, when those wonderful Aurora monster models were all the rage. Along with *Famous Monsters of Filmland Magazine,* the models are what I remember most about my boyhood during the late '60s and early '70s. Those cardboard boxes of plastic fodder for my ghoulish pre-pubescent imagination.

Aurora started releasing the Universal Monster models in the early '60s, in what was known as the "long box." That was before my time. Sure, I watched the old monster movies on my local creature feature around that time, but it wasn't until later—around 1969 or 1970—when I really got into building the models. And they were the "glow-in-the-dark" kind in the square box.

I received a very modest allowance back then for doing chores around the house and it was a flat-out miracle, but I usually managed to save every penny until we went to town at the start of the following month (that's what folks did when they lived out in the country with the big city twenty or thirty miles away). I remember riding in the back seat of my father's old two-toned '56 Chevy, sticking my hand in my jeans pocket every now and then to make sure I had remembered to bring those few dollar bills and a jingling fistful of change. If had forgotten my loot, it would have been a dark and dismal journey indeed. But luckily I never did, for that particular trip to town was motivated (on my part) by thoughts of glorious monsters, both on the printed page of a magazine and in styrene plastic within a creepily packaged box.

After stopping at Brown's Drugstore for the latest issue of *Famous Monsters,* we would head over to the only Sears department store in Nashville at the time. That was before the days of the big shopping malls... if you wanted to shop, you pretty much had to go downtown. Sandwiched between the mail-order pickup and the lawn and garden department was the toy department. Sears had an entire back wall devoted to models and hobby supplies back then. Most of the models were hot rods and military aircraft, but stuck smack-dab in the center of all the "normal stuff," as my dad would call it, were the Aurora monster models... those square boxes bearing every man-made monster, vampire, werewolf, and creature that I had ever loved.

After selecting my monster-of-choice for that particular month, I would add some model glue (yes, they actually allowed kids to buy the stuff without a parent's permission at that time) and maybe a few bottles of Testor's paint if needed. I never cared much for the shiny paint, preferring the muted tones instead, for added authenticity. Also, I never smeared my monsters fangs and claws with candy-apple red to simulate blood. A lot of guys I knew wanted their monsters extra gory (even Kong and Godzilla), but I made mine as close to their movie counterparts as possible. This annoyed my model-building pals, but then I always did tend to go against the grain for the sake of realism.

On the way home, I always pestered my parents to let me peel away the cellophane and open the box. My mother insisted that I wait until we got home, but she knew the suspense was killing me! "Okay," she'd finally give in, "but if you lose a piece in the car, I don't want to hear you bellyache about it later." Fortunately, I never lost a single piece of a model kit… even when my father slammed on the brakes at stop signs, because he wasn't paying attention.

We would usually get home around one or two o'clock in the afternoon. I'd take refuge in my bedroom, crack the window for proper ventilation (even in the dead of winter) and, with a snack of Kool-Aid and a peanut butter sandwich, prepare to work on my most recent model project. Most of the time, I would have an issue of *Famous Monsters* laid open for inspiration, but not close enough to be soiled by stray globs of glue or paint (heaven forbid!) On the glow-in-the-dark models, sometimes I used the glow pieces, sometimes I didn't. The models came with both sets of heads, hands, and feet, giving you a choice. If you wanted, you could even take the extra pieces and construct a cool, little "mini-monster."

My favorite of the bunch was the Creature from the Black Lagoon. He was cast in green plastic, so there wasn't a whole lot of painting involved, just the belly scales, gills, and fins. The Gillman had a really cool base, too, which included a skeleton hand, a swamp snake on a gnarled tree branch, and a big spiny lizard that I never could quite identify. A lot of the other models had neat bases as well. The Mummy's had chunks of temple columns and pyramid blocks decorated with hieroglyphics and a king cobra. Godzilla's had the buildings of Tokyo underfoot and Kong's had a totally-trampled jungle scene. Perhaps my favorite base was the Phantom's. There were the usual garnishments like rats and such, but there was also the window of a dungeon with a rotting and horrified victim within, clutching the iron bars in desperation. The least remarkable base belonged to Frankenstein. It was simply a grassy cemetery plot with a tombstone at the rear. Pretty boring compared to the others, but that didn't matter. You simply *had* to have ol' Square-Head in your collection.

A few of the models sort of irked me in one way or another. I loved the Wolfman, but could never figure out why he wore no shirt! After all, Lon Chaney, Jr. always donned a long-sleeved work shirt whenever he went through the change. If it hadn't been for his jeans, held up by a rope (another faux pas of realism on the model designer's part), he would have been naked as a jaybird! Also, the Hunchback model was sort of a sloppy mixture of Chaney, Sr.'s rendition and Anthony Quinn's bell ringer. And the Dr. Jekyll as Mr. Hyde model was several inches smaller than all the others, although it did have a cool table with laboratory beakers and bottles, and an overturned stool. The Witch was the most disappointing of the bunch. The figure itself was only about four or five inches tall, compared to Frankie's impressive nine inches. The Witch did have the most elaborate base of all, though, with a boiling cauldron and lots of creepy details that were particularly hard to paint.

One of my favorite models wasn't even a true Universal monster at all. The Forgotten Prisoner of Castel Mare was the partly-clothed skeleton of some unfortunate victim, shackled to a moldering dungeon wall, its jaws stretched wide in a silent scream. Any youthful lover of horror really dug skeletons (pardon my pun) so that probably contributed to the Forgotten Prisoner's appeal, even though it didn't actually originate from a real motion picture. I heard later that it was created exclusively for *Famous Monsters Magazine,* which made it even more desirable.

The sad part was, once you finally put together the original twelve Aurora models, there were no more to be found, except for maybe the Munsters and the superhero models like Superman, Batman, and Robin. But just having those twelve horrific monsters on your bookshelf, glowing eerily in the dark hours of the night was both chilling and comforting to us monster-loving boys.

In recent years, companies like Revell, Polar Lights, and Moebius have re-released most of the old Aurora models. For decades, there was a disheartening rumor that Jekyll & Hyde's original molds had been destroyed, but the 2007 re-issue by Moebius proved that urban myth to be false. Although today's youth aren't really into model-building like their parents (or grandparents) were, and most kids wouldn't know Count Dracula if he came up and sank his fangs into their throat, the new re-issues give model-builders, both old and new, the chance to construct their favorite movie monster and relive those nostalgic days from the monster boom of the Sixties and Seventies.

– October 2011

About the Author

Ronald Kelly was born November 20, 1959 in Nashville, Tennessee. He attended Pegram Elementary School and Cheatham County Central High School, and had aspirations of become a comic book artist before his interests turned to writing fiction.

Ronald Kelly began his professional writing career in the horror genre in 1986 with his first short story, "Breakfast Serial". to *Terror Time Again* magazine. Specializing in tales of Southern-Fried horror, his work was widely published in magazines such as *Deathrealm, Grue, New Blood,* and *Cemetery Dance.* His first novel, Hindsight was released by Zebra Books in 1990. He wrote for Zebra for six years, publishing such novels as *Fear, Blood Kin,* and *Moon of the Werewolf (Undertaker's Moon).* His audiobook collection, *Dark Dixie: Tales of Southern Horror,* was included on the nominating ballot of the 1992 Grammy Awards for Best Spoken Word or Non-Musical Album. Ronald's short fiction work has been published in major anthologies such as *Cold Blood, Borderlands 3, Dark at Heart, Shock Rock, Hot Blood: Seeds of Fear,* and many more,

After selling hundreds of thousands of books, the bottom dropped out of the mass-market horror market in 1996. When Zebra dropped their horror line in October 1996, Ronald Kelly stopped writing for ten years and worked various jobs including welder, factory worker, production manager, drugstore manager, and custodian. In 2006, Ronald Kelly began writing again. In early 2008,

Croatoan Publishing released his work Flesh Welder as a stand-alone chapbook, and it quickly sold out. In early 2009 Cemetery Dance Publications released a limited-edition hardcover of his first short story collection, *Midnight Grinding & Other Twilight Terrors.* Also in 2010, Cemetery Dance released his first novel in over ten years, *Hell Hollow,* as a limited edition hardcover. Ronald's Zebra/Pinnacle horror novels were released in limited hardcover editions by Thunderstorm Books as *The Essential Ronald Kelly series.* Each book contained a new novella related to the novel's original storyline.

During his comeback to the horror genre, he has written several additional novels, such as *Restless Shadows* and *The Buzzard Zone,* as well as numerous short story collections: *After the Burn, Mister Glow-Bones & Other Halloween Tales, The Halloween Store & Other Tales of All-Hallows' Eve, Season's Creepings: Tales of Holiday Horror, Irish Gothic,* and *The Web of La Sanguinaire & Other Arachnid Horrors.* In 2021, his collection of extreme horror stories, *The Essential Sick Stuff,* published by Silver Shamrock Publications, won the Splatterpunk Award for Best Collection.

Ronald Kelly currently lives in a backwoods hollow in Brush Creek, Tennessee, with his wife and young'uns, and a nervous Jack Russell terrier named Toby, who is the physical incarnation of Courage the Cowardly Dog.

CROSSROAD
PRESS

Made in the USA
Las Vegas, NV
26 April 2023